DANCING ON HORSES

TONY J. STAFFORD

iUniverse®

DANCING ON HORSES

iUniverse books may be ordered through booksellers or by contacting:

iUniverse
1663 Liberty Drive
Bloomington, IN 47403
www.iuniverse.com
1-800-Authors (1-800-288-4677)

ISBN: 978-1-5320-4639-1 (sc)
ISBN: 978-1-5320-4638-4 (e)

Library of Congress Control Number: 2018904963

Print information available on the last page.

iUniverse rev. date: 04/20/2018

PROLOGUE

North Carolina, BC (Before Civil Rights Act)

White. The colorless color. The background color for other colors, especially to black, as on the printed page. Without white, black would not be possible; without black, white would have nothing to say. White is the absence of color—and character.

White. In winter, there is snow that can be ubiquitously white with icy-white ponds; in summer, there is the whiteness of a crystal sun covering the green earth with a bright glare; there are the white moon and stars that create a white earth and white shadows at night; there is the whiteness of concrete buildings, sidewalks, steeples on Baptist churches, clapboard houses, government buildings, city halls, and convertible cars; in schools, there is white chalk on blackboards (subjugation, not conjugation); in spring, there are the white dogwood blossoms adorning the woods, as well as gardenias and hydrangeas dominating lawns; white apple blossoms, white cherry blossoms, plum blossoms, and other white fruit-tree blossoms dance for miles in the spring breezes; white roses punctuate flower gardens, and white clover blankets the yards; in fall, white chrysanthemums rejoice and reign; in winter, white pansies assert themselves through the white snow of February.

There is white flour, white buttermilk, and white lard to make brown biscuits baked in a white oven and served on white china and eaten with shiny silverware; white are raw potatoes, raw turnips, raw onions, and raw milk kept in a white refrigerator; the rest of the kitchen gleams with white. There are white sheets and white bedspreads in bedrooms, white towels in bathrooms, white sofas and chairs in the living room, and white wrought iron furniture on the porch. All the wooden houses are painted white to nestle their white occupants.

There are white teachers in white schools, white preachers in white churches, white professors in white universities, white members in white country clubs (being waited on by blacks), white judges in white courts, white mayors and white council members in white city halls, white police officers enforcing white laws, white politicians running white governments, all in the interests of whites. Publicly there are toilets for whites only, white-only drinking fountains, white seating sections on public transports, white sports teams, white picture shows for white audiences in white movie houses, white crowds at all public events, instituted by and for whites: mid-twentieth-century North Carolina, a white world legally, while black is seen mutely in the shadows.

Tobe Stanhope was bred in and took his being from that white world, which for him was a small cotton textile mill town, Belhaven, on the outer shoulders of Charlotte with its tall, gleaming white buildings. White cotton fibers swirled all around the little town, landing in shrubs, trees, lawns, and roadways, and the textile workers trudged home every day wearing white cotton remnants on their overalls. For most, it was a constricted world, consisting of labor in the cotton mills and daily humbling in small white houses huddled together in the mill villages owned by the cotton-mill millionaires, begetting more future cotton-mill laborers in those same houses and churching in all-white churches under white steeples on Sundays with the choirs in white robes and the altars decorated with white lilies. Tobe never knew a single colored student in school, not to mention Hispanic or Asian, even though coloreds formed a significant but silent slice of the population.

CHAPTER 1

Belhaven, North Carolina, 1947

"Daddy?" Tobe's father was looking into the mirror over the sink in the bathroom while Tobe stood in the bathroom doorway. His father made it a habit of often looking in the mirror for lots of different reasons. His dad slowly gained consciousness and words.

"Yes, son?" His dad turned to look at him, shaving cream covering the bottom half of his face like a white surgical mask. The white cream made his teeth look browner than usual. After another suspenseful hiatus of silence, he asked, "What is it?"

Twelve-year-old Tobe was standing outside the open bathroom door in a little square hall that was the center of their smallish house and from which other rooms radiated. "Can I ..." Tobe hesitated, trying to find words and courage.

"I'm waitin'," his father said, which helped Tobe lose his self-consciousness and find his voice.

"Can I ast you a question?"

"I thought you had something important to say." His father continued scraping his face, the relentless razor mowing off the stubble scratchily. Rebuffed and slightly unnerved, Tobe turned to saunter away.

"Wait a minute."

Tobe stopped.

"Come back here," the father commanded. "Sorry, son. I just don't want to be late for church. In my book, if you ain't a half hour early, you're late. What'd you wanna ast me?"

"Oh, nut'in."

"No, no. Come on. Ast me."

"I was just wonderin'—"

"Yes?"

"Wull, you know how they're always talkin' in church about—you know—usin' the word 'saved,' talkin' 'bout 'bein' saved.' I was just wonderin'—"

His daddy had finished wiping the shaving cream from his face and was now facing Tobe in his Jockey underwear, his ample belly swaying downward.

"Go on."

"I was just wonderin' what they mean by 'bein' saved.'" Tobe, in his hesitancy, made his voice barely audible.

Tobe's dad stared in silence, appearing to process how to proceed while he splashed Mennen's aftershave lotion amply on his face and neck, as well as under his arms. Tobe associated the familiar astringent odor with his father, while at the moment his eyes watered with freshness.

"Who told you to ast me this?" His father's bushy dark eyebrows lowered at his own question and intimidated Tobe.

"Nobody," Tobe insouciantly answered.

"Are you sure?" his father asked as he dabbed his face with Tobe's mother's powder puff. His father and his mother believed strongly that a shiny face made one look as though he had just finished plowing a field on the farm, a shiny face being closely akin to having a red neck.

"Yessir."

"Where'd you hear such a thaing?" His father suddenly had time to cross-examine him. "Follow me," his father said as he turned to go through the bedroom door and into the bedroom where Tobe's mother stood in front of a full-length dresser mirror (Tobe often pondered the fact that there were so many mirrors in his parents' house).

Tobe's mother was dressed in a smart pink two-piece suit, with dark stockings, red high-heels, and a small rakish red hat with one long pink feather. His mother was a slightly dark-complexioned white woman, by comparison to the white world around them, with brown eyes, brown hair, and brown hands (Tobe had his mother's skin tone); she had thin lips and a white smile with a sliver of gold between the two front teeth. She was slender and carried herself rigidly with as much dignity as she could muster, sang nasally in the church choir, taught children's Sunday school, and carried her Bible lovingly and proudly.

In the conversation that followed, Tobe's father proceeded to dress himself, putting on his freshly starched shirt (complaining about "never enough starch"); adding his navy-blue pin-striped suit pants, his black silk socks, and his black shiny wing tips; and finally tying his red-and-black tie. While Tobe's parents were working-class mill hands with modest incomes, when it came to dressing up for church, they looked as though they worked on Wall Street. Also, his mother's collection of hats always awed little Tobe, for she always looked as though she were going to the Kentucky Derby, a southern tradition Tobe had heard about. His parents tried heartily to impress God. They also never wanted it to be said about them that they were not taking their religion seriously, nor did they wish to run the risk of becoming victims of behind-the-hand whispering, which could happen over the slightest misplaced hair or overlooked smudge somewhere. It struck Tobe that people could be so tiny-minded, and church could sometimes be a mean place.

"Are you sure somebody didn't put you up to this?" His father huffed on his black shoes as he rubbed them with his shoe rag, trying to make them even shinier. "Like maybe your brother?"

"No, sir—er—yessir, I'm sure." Tobe was thinking, *what have I got myself into here?* while looking for a way to escape.

"I see." His father dissected the situation.

"Hey, Daddy, it's okay. It's no big deal. Just curious; that's all," Tobe said, backing toward the door like a horse backing out of a stall. "I need to go git ready so we won't be late."

"We got a minute." His father combed his lustrous black hair.

"No, really—it's okay.'"

"Sump'n's happenin'."

"Sir?"

"Sump'n's happenin' with you. I can tell."

"What?"

"That's what I wanna find out. Let's get to the bottom of this," he said as he fiddled with his windsor knot and then flipped the ends of his tie through it.

Tobe wasn't sure what to say. "I just wanted to know what they meant by—"

"Jesus has got you in his grip." He pulled his windsor knot tightly up to his stiff collar.

"Huh?"

"Jesus is workin' on your soul right now. You better not fight it." He held his suit coat up to brush it with his clothes brush.

"I ain't—"

"Give yourself up to Jesus." He now had his suit coat on and was standing in front of the full-length mirror, admiring his handsome figure (which was Tobe's assessment of his father's view of himself). Tobe knew what was next.

"How do I look?"

"Fightin'—"

"I said, 'How do I look?'" Daddy preened and leaned, Tobe could tell, into self-satisfaction.

"Fine."

"Jesus is convictin' you of sin right now." He gathered up his Bible and Sunday school literature.

"Sin?"

"We're goin' to go talk to the preacher." He turned to the mother and asked, "You ready?"

Tobe felt as though he were being buoyed along in a roiling brook without anything to grasp to save himself—no tree branches, no boulders, no banks, nothing—just him and the powerful current taking him he knew not where, perhaps even out to the boundless sea. He would have that feeling often for the rest of the day.

In the car, Tobe thought about his family's roots and his identity. He was aware that he was the product of a long line of red-clay dirt farmers on his father's side, who in their uneducated way saw nothing amiss in their white world, except their own impoverishment. They were humble folk, driven into subjugation by generations of poverty; soul-wrenching, mind-binding labor; and an incalculable amount of contention with a life in which there were no victors. They were a defeated people without realizing it and toiled on and remained poor. His own parents' generation left the tenant farms and entered the factories, left the sweet earth to become routinized and mechanized but with a paycheck—such as it was. It was an advancement, as they saw it.

As for his own parents, the blandness of their lives, which they were blissfully unaware of, was seasoned with religion, not just a gentle acknowledgment of its flavor but an obsessive craving that was slaked by almost daily attendance at church: Sunday school, Sunday-morning worship service, baptismal events, Sunday-afternoon church conferences, Sunday-evening Baptist Training Union, Sunday-evening worship service, Wednesday-night prayer meeting, choir rehearsal, Saturday-night cottage prayer meeting, religious encampments, and biannual revival meetings, not to mention their own daily devotions in their own home and countless visitations to the individuals who were lost and damned in order to witness to them. Religion centered their lives.

Tobe often suspected that his parents kept him in church as much as possible as a way of keeping him away from temptation, even though he often met numerous girls through the church-related activities— which led to zero sexual activity. Tobe thought that maybe his father's compulsive religious activities also harnessed his own physical urges.

East Belhaven Baptist Church was located, naturally enough, in the east sector of Belhaven at the end of a humble shopping strip on one side of East Catawba Street with the Majestic (ironically named) cotton mill on the opposite side of the street. In fact, numerous cotton mills dotted and ringed the neighborhood with names like the Aberfoyle, the Chronicle, the Acme, the Crescent, and, unbelievably, the Climax. Every mill, which was owned principally and separately by two wealthy families who lived in mansions, was surrounded by the "mill village" where the workers lived in cramped, squalid houses. Everyone identified his or herself by the mill village in which they lived, such as, "I'm from the Climax," or, "I live on the Majestic." A large number of the congregation of East Belhaven Baptist lived in the mill villages.

Tobe's dad parked their Model A Ford on, naturally enough, Church Street, and the family exited from four separate doors and scattered, except Tobe's father, who yanked Tobe along while Tobe peered up at the expansive church. The building was composed of dark red brick with stained glass windows, a high porch approached by wide, concrete steps with tall white columns (Doric actually), and a steeple pointing upward at the front of the roof (many Southern Baptist churches were built in the style of St. Martins-in-the-Field in the middle of London, which has no field in sight). Tobe remembered the story of how the East Belhaven Church had been built toward the beginning of the twentieth century by the members of the church, with their own hands and simple tools, putting in hours in the dark, lighted by lanterns, after working in the mills all day and on weekends. Tobe and his dad entered through the large double doors, crossed the vestibule, and went into the sanctuary. They walked down the aisle between rows of black theater-style seats (Tobe had been told that pews were too Catholic), neared a raised dais and pulpit behind the offering table (in a Catholic church, it would be called an altar) down front, with a railed choir section to the pulpit's right side, a baptismal pool behind the pulpit, and a door on the left side that led to classrooms and the preacher's "study," to which place Tobe's father was marshalling him.

After his father told the preacher the story, with some distortions, about their conversation as they were getting ready for church, Reverend Hicks leaned back in his swivel chair, folded his hands across his ample belly while twiddling his thumbs, and looked piously at the ceiling, as though he were beseeching heaven. Reverend B. S. (Bertrand Stanley) Hicks had a shiny dome for a head with a fringe of gray around the edge, gold-rimmed glasses that matched his gold tooth, and a gold watch chain across his vested, bulging torso. Reverend Hicks was seated at his oak roll-top desk (with swivel chair), the father was ensconced in front of a bookshelf stocked full of fundamentalist tomes (one of which possessed a detailed description of what heaven looks like, along with its exact square mileage), and Tobe was placed diametrically opposite from his father in front of another crammed bookshelf. It could be an office, except for the books, in any business, with no crucifixes, no crosses, no saints, no religious images, and not even a picture of Jesus. It was the office of a Southern Baptist preacher where, in direct revolt against Catholicism, man-made religious images were banished because of their idolatry. After all, it was the Baptists' belief that the Catholic Church was merely a political institution and the pope was the Antichrist, and they were dwelling in the land of, or the office of, the "priesthood of the believer," a shibboleth and mantra of the Southern Baptist Church.

"Do you know what it takes to be saved?" The very tone of the preacher's voice made it clear that he had asked this question untold times and that he was even doubting whether he should ask it anymore, especially of a twelve-year-old boy who had only a dim consciousness of conscience. It sounded as though the preacher felt that he was wasting his time and should be working on his sermon—yes, even, or especially, at nine thirty on a Sunday morning.

A silence ensued, except for the ticking of the big clock sitting atop the preacher's roll-top desk. Tobe wasn't sure what the answer was but assumed that the preacher wanted to preachify in order to earn his salary, so Tobe gave the correct answer, "No, sir," and the reverend proceeded to seermonize for the next fifteen minutes. Tobe hardly heard a word of it, and what he did hear, he did not understand, but he nodded at appropriate intervals and gave verbal sounds in the spaces of the preacher's well-timed pauses. What Tobe mostly heard was his inner voice: *What am I going to order for Sunday dinner at the restaurant?* he thought for a moment. *But coconut pie for sure,* and then his mind darted on: *I wonder where me and Buddy can go bike riding this afternoon. We ain't been to the creek in a while.* His attention returned to the reverend's tedious words, briefly (later in college, when studying Shakespeare, he will come across Hotspur's description of Owen Glendower as "tedious as a tired horse" and think of Reverend Hicks), and then wandered on: *I wonder if the pretty girl with the auburn curls and green eyes will be in Sunday school class this morning.* And then he saw her dimly in his memory and felt a pleasantly warm and tingly sensation between his legs, in contrast to the pain and boredom that daunted his ears by the preacher's words, far more enticing than the present discussion of "being saved."

"You understand what I'm saying?" the preacher said as he leaned forward in his squeaky chair. Reverent Hicks stared hard at Tobe with an earnest expression on his face. And then he waited.

"Oh, yessir, yessir, I understand completely," Tobe said.

"Good. Okay. I want you to get down on your knees now, right there in front of your chair." The reverend then turned to Tobe's daddy. "And you too, Winston—right there in front of your chair will be fine. I'd join you two, but my knees won't let me."

Nor will your fat belly, Tobe thought as he pictured the obese parson on his knees, unable to get up, and snickered.

"What are you laughing about?" the preacher barked at Tobe. "This is serious business."

"I know, sir. I know." Tobe tried his hardest to sound serious and sanctimonious.

"Then what are you snickering about?"

Tobe tried to think. "I—"

"Yes?"

"I just suddenly felt real happy, that's all." Tobe quickly got to his knees while his daddy, giving Tobe a damning look, did the same.

"Ah," the reverend said with a tone of approval. "That's a sign that Jesus has come into your heart and filled you with the joy of the Holy Spirit. That's a sure sign that you have been saved. Amen. Praise God. Let's pray."

Reverend Hicks then droned on according to form about suffering the little children to come "unto Me—for such is the kingdom of heaven"—and how precious every soul is, no matter how young and innocent, because we are all corrupted by Adam's sin against God. Tobe could not help wondering why God needed to be told all this and thought about the copper-haired girl in his Sunday school class again, or, even better, the picture of Jane Russell in the *Charlotte Observer* advertising the reshowing of *The Outlaw* with her braless blouse, enormous breasts, insufficient small shorts, and her long legs. Finally, Tobe heard the word "amen" and opened his eyes, thinking, *Thank God. My knees are killing me.* Tobe and his father both stood up, his father offering his hand to the minister in gratitude.

"We have a baptismal scheduled for this evening's worship service. Tobe can be baptized tonight," the preacher said.

Tobe froze like a marble statue. *What have I gotten myself into now?* he wondered again.

"That's great," Daddy said to the preacher, enthusiastically shaking his hand.

Reverend Hicks turned to Tobe. "This morning after my sermon is over and we have the invitational hymn, you'll come down to the front to make your public confession of faith."

Tobe could not breathe. His legs felt dead, his hands and arms ached with pain, his heart riveted while his brain buzzed, and he thought, *I can't go through with this—this—this—pretending. All I wanted to know was what they meant by "being saved. That is not what I meant at all. That is not it, at all"* he thought, unaware that he was echoing "The Love Song of J. Alfred Prufrock." He sensed that he had violated some sacred creed that he did not believe in and was not a part of, that he was being hypocritical, and he worried about how God was going to punish him for lying and pretending. The terror he owned was so great that he felt like the inside of his skin consisted of millions of needles, squeezing in on him and pricking his insides, and so unbearable was the pain that he was certain he was going to faint, even though he had never fainted before.

As they left the preacher's study, Tobe started off in a different direction from his father, who said, "Where ya goin'?"

"I'm just goin' to run over to the church library to pick up a couple of books." Tobe's one passion of his childhood, amidst all the religion, was reading—his escape, his refuge, his enrichment, if one could call *The Hardy Boys* enrichment. Reading was one of the constant pleasures of his childhood.

"Don't be late for Sunday school."

"I won't," Tobe assured him.

Ever since he was ten or eleven years old, he had spent many long summer afternoons home alone while his parents and his brother worked, reading in the lounge chair in their den while munching a peanut butter and jelly sandwich which was blessed by a glass of milk. Their church had a library with secular books as well, like The Hardy Boys series, which Tobe went through with a single-mindedness. Every Sunday morning, Tobe would return a stack of books and then spend a pleasurable, brief time browsing through the bookshelves looking for more books, discovering all kinds of juvenile literature in addition to *The Hardy Boys*, such as *Tim Bolton, Flying Midshipman, Nancy Drew,* Judy Bolton mysteries (yes, a little outside the realm of his taste but still enjoyable), *Charlotte's Web,* books by James Fenimore Cooper, *Anne of Green Gables, The Once and Future King, The Legend of Sleepy Hollow, The Prince and the Pauper, A Tale of Two Cities, The Three Musketeers,* and graduating to the edge of good literature, such as the short stories of Edgar Allen Poe and the young-adult works of Mark

Twain, such as *Huckleberry Finn* and *Tom Sawyer*. It was several deliciously dizzing summers for him, and they planted deep within him a love that could never be extinguished. Reading provided Tobe a pleasurable respite from oppressive religiosity.

The tradition in the Southern Baptist Church is that in order to complete all the necessary steps in God's plan of salvation, one must make a public confession of faith, another shibboleth, which means that after the sermon is over and the congregation and choir are singing the "Hymn of Invitation," one must make that trip down the aisle (in the olden days of tent revivals, it was known as "the sawdust trail" where they "jerked 'em to Jesus") to the altar where the preacher stands waiting to receive the born-again sinner, whereupon, after the hymn is finished, the preacher has the audience sit down so that he can herald the new convert.

On this particular Sunday, after the preacher finished his sermon, he took up his hymn book and said, "Let's all turn in our hymnal to page fifty-seven, 'Jesus Is Calling,' and I know that in fact Jesus is calling someone here today. I say to this person, please come down and confess your sins, ask God for forgiveness, and enter the kingdom of heaven. Let us sing."

The choir led off with, "Jesus is tenderly calling thee home, Calling today, Calling today, Why from the sunshine of love wilt thou roam / Farther and farther away," and then came the chorus repeating "calling today" over and over.

Tobe was paralyzed, barely able to breathe, and then he started hyperventilating. He could not take that first step and was gripping the seat in front of him with a desperate, iron grip. The hymn went on, stanza after stanza, "Jesus is waiting, oh come to him now, Jesus is pleading, O list to his voice," and still Tobe was unable to move. The hymn ended, and the preacher silently surveyed the congregation. Tobe noted the tension emanating from the people around him and heard faint whisperings. Everyone continued standing and waiting.

"Let's turn in our hymnals to page thirty-seven, 'There Is a Fountain Filled with Blood.' I am going to ask the organist to play this hymn softly for just a minute before we sing. There is a member of our congregation that I talked with this morning, and I know that this person became convicted of his sins, accepted Jesus as his personal savior, and became a born-again soul. I want everybody, while we sing this hymn, to pray that this sinner will find the courage to step out and follow Jesus. That's all it takes is that first step, and then you'll be on your way to salvation. Choir." Reverend Hicks seemed determined to meet his quota for the month, for a Southern Baptist minister's effectiveness is judged by the number souls he saves and the size of his church membership—as well as the amount in the offering plate.

"There is a fountain filled with blood," the choir and congregation sang together. "Drawn from Immanuel's veins; And sinners plunged beneath that flood, Lose all their guilty stains." Tobe was seated only a few rows from the front, on the end of his row next to the aisle, and he could hear his mother's voice in the choir above all the others, nasally vocalizing louder than all the rest, as though she were singing directly to her son, which he knew she was.

Tobe's older brother leaned over to him and said, "Go on, dummy. I'm gittin hungry. They're waitin' for you." Just as Tobe was about to say, "I can't," his brother gave him a shove that pushed Tobe into the aisle, where he lost his balance and fell on the red carpet.

The preached waddled up the aisle, shouting, "God be praised! God be praised! Glory hallelujah! God be praised!" Reverend Hicks picked Tobe up and whispered, "I thought you'd never come." He firmly pulled him down the aisle to the front, where he turned to the congregation and said, "God works in mysterious ways. Praise be to God."

After that, Tobe never heard another word the preacher said, being numb, embarrassed, and bruised. And he never got an answer to his original question, "What does it mean to be saved?"

In the car immediately after church on their way to Couples Grill, Tobe was still thinking about coconut pie instead of salvation. The first car that Tobe's family could afford to buy in 1947 (they had been without an automobile ever since his parents were married, getting around mostly on bicycles and depending on rides from other people) was a used Model T Ford, vintage unknown but probably about twenty years old (Tobe observed that they often had to use a crank, inserted just under the radiator, to start it). They then upgraded to a used Model A, about fifteen years old (they were desperately trying to move up to the burgeoning middle class of post–World War II). They were in the Model A on this day after church, taking themselves to a restaurant in their *own* car, without having to ask anyone for a ride. Everyone's pride was in place, except for Tobe's.

"Cat got your tongue?" his father asked, looking in the rearview mirror at Tobe, who remained silent. "How you feelin'?" The eyes in the rearview mirror glared at him.

His brother punched him on the arm. "Answer Daddy."

"Aw right."

"Aw right? That's all? You just entered the kingdom of heaven, and you just feel aw right?"

Tobe felt miserable, confused, and fraudlent, like the phony he knew he was. He felt as though he had deceived his father, the preacher, the whole congregation—but mostly himself. He still did not know what it meant to be saved, and yet he had gone through this whole traumatic event. He felt as though he needed a bath, which the baptismal would take care of, the thought of which further distressed him.

One of Tobe's favorite things of the whole week was the Sunday dinner out (in the old agrarian South, as in the Elizabethan era, dinner was the midday meal, while the evening meal was supper). This one was ruined. They traveled to the restaurant on Wilkerson Boulevard, a modern, for them, four-lane highway, crossed the wide Catawba River, passed all the bars and taverns on the Charlotte side of the river (awaiting the traffic from Tobe's adjoining dry county), and motored for about ten miles to the cuff on Charlotte's sleeve.

As their old Model A Ford entered the parking lot of Couples Grill, Tobe began to feel nauseated, and the thought of food, even coconut pie, made it worse, but he knew he had to see it through. Everyone exited the car into the bright sunshine of an exceptionally fine North Carolina spring day, except for Tobe, who was having trouble opening the aged door of the car, mainly because he did not have the will to push the handle far enough. His brother, already outside, opened the door for him from the other side, saying, "Come on, dummy. I told you I'm starving." Tobe complied.

The restaurant was crowded with churchgoers, chirping, laughing, gossiping, taking off the robes of righteousness that they had donned for church. It was an ordinary restaurant with Formica tables, plastic-covered chairs, red-and-black square-tiled floors, and numerous tables and chairs. And it was crowded. To Tobe and his family, it was luxurious; to anyone with a wider frame of reference, it was barely pedestrian. In addition to the noise, the smell of food worsened Tobe's condition.

The family members slid into a cushiony booth, were greeted by the waitress with water glasses, menus, and crackers, and fell into the silence of menu reading. Tobe did not really need to read the menu, for he had known what he wanted from the time he thought about it in the minister's office. Looking up at the waitress when his turn came, Tobe committed, "I'll have the fried pork chops, mashed potatoes and gravy, and black-eyed peas. And coconut pie for dessert." He normally had a robust appetite, but it seemed to have left him, and he wondered, *How am I ever going to get through this meal?*

His parents always ordered the same thing, "Southern fried chicken, white meat only, and iced sweet tea." His brother, who had a repulsion to chicken (having watched his grandmother kill too many of them), ordered a meatless meal with lots of cherry Jell-O and desserts.

The conversation between his mother and father consisted of a critical review of serious ecclesiastical matters while Tobe made mental notes: Maude had too many feathers in her stupid-looking hat; the dress Nelly wore was totally out of style; the dress young Gail Brown had on was way too revealing; Frances's husband, Ralph, had a bad case of diarrhea; that worthless Frank Carpenter was out of work again; Joanne suspected her husband of having an affair; and the poisonous enemies, Carl and Sam, sat poisonously glaring at each other in true Southern Baptist hypocritical fashion during preaching.

Tobe noted that nobody was safe, but the most salacious story that got his attention was about Rose Rumfelt, whose husband, Earl, had promised to fix their neighbor Sara Stowe's toilet one evening after work, as promised, but Earl had to work late and couldn't make the appointment; consequently, Rose decided to walk over and give her neighbor Sara the message about her husband, and when Sara answered the door, she was totally nude in expectation of Earl coming over. The comments circulating through the church were gleefully indulgent, such as "talk about being caught bare handed," or "being caught with your pants down," or "finding the naked truth," or "quoting the tenth commandment: 'thou shalt not covet thy neighbor's wife.'" It almost rivaled the latest gossip about the church's attractive divorcee who recently got pregnant by the visiting revivalist preacher (such was the "advent" after every revivalist preacher left town). Tobe took it all in.

Tobe listened vaguely while other matters dwelt in his mind.

And then his father said, "Let's say a blessing and thank God for His goodness." Tobe wondered if they had not prayed enough for one morning.

The smell of the food that the waitress brought to the table brought Tobe's mind back to his most urgent problem, the eating of a big meal. Fried pork chops had never smelled so greasy before, mashed potatoes and gravy never looked so much like slop, and the black-eyed peas, his favorite of all foods, were at best neutral. Like most preteen boys, Tobe had a shocking capacity for food; he had been known to eat five of his mother's hamburgers and gravy at a single sitting, augmented with a couple of slices of coconut cake, all accompanied by a half gallon of milk. This was not that day as he stared in wonder at the amount of food in front of him. Tobe braced himself and took his first bite of pork chop, followed by a scoop of potatoes and a couple of peas, and then repeated the sequence several times. The food had no flavor, but he chewed and swallowed and was encouraged by both parents to clean his plate "because there are people in China that are starvin'." Tobe wondered how eating his meal would help the Chinese.

It started somewhere deep down in areas he did not even know he possessed, a strange stirring, a punch in the gut, and then a tidal wave of full-blown nausea. There was no controlling it, and he felt it rising up from the bottom of his stomach into his chest as though he were walking deeper and deeper into a pond. His body shivered, and then came the explosion in his throat and the relentless outpouring from his mouth. The first wave landed in his lap, the next one on the booth seat, followed by the next all over the floor. His brother's profound commentary was, "Yuck."

Daddy slapped his napkin on the table, stomped his hoof, and soared into a tirade, beginning with "Look what you've done. You've gone and ruined my dinner and everybody else's. What's wrong with you?" It seemed as though everyone in the restaurant was looking at their table.

"Cain't you see we're in a public restaurant? You've embarrassed your whole family." He turned to the rest of the diners and said, "I'm sorry. You'll have to forgive him," and then turned back to Tobe. "You're just tryin' to git attention. You want people to feel sorry for you, that's all, but it ain't workin'."

By this time, the waitress had brought in the mop mob, who went about their business. "You've also ruined your Sunday best," he mumbled as he waited for the mop cops to finish. "Let's git outta here." He rose along with everyone else and then grabbed Tobe hurtfully by the arm and hissed, "I'm on to the little game you're playing, but like it or not, you're going to be baptized tonight."

While Tobe was unable to actually describe what was going on inside of him, what he was experiencing was extreme guilt, not over the restaurant regurgitation but over the fraud he felt he was birthing. He was going to be baptized, and he still did not know what it meant to be saved or to be baptized, even though he had witnessed countless baptisms in his short lifetime. When the family arrived home from the restaurant, he went straight to his room and shut the door, telling his brother that he needed to be alone, a necessary explanation since they shared the space, and proceeded to peel off his Sunday outfit and don some weekday clothes.

Alone, he sat in the rocker in their bedroom, uncomfortable though it was with its pink, quilted cushions, and scanned his environment while trying to get into the right mood. He looked at the frilly, sheer curtains over the windows (totally inappropriate for a boy's quarters), the fancy bedspread on the bed (appropriate for an adult-inhabited manor house), the cherry wood four-poster bed, chest of drawers, nightstand, and dresser (Tobe remembered that his father, while a blue-collar worker, believed that good furniture was an investment, and he had a knack for driving a hard bargain at the furniture store), and the walls decorated with nature pictures from the local five-and-dime and, of all things, a cheap copy of Thomas Gainsborough's *The Blue Boy*, as though that alone would compensate for the senior citizen décor of the place. Tobe understood that his mother had an image of what a beautiful, well-appointed bedroom should look like—from a woman's perspective—but Tobe did not share her vision. She did not once stop to consider the fact that the space was for boys, and even if she had, she would not have known what was appropriate, being one of twelve sisters. Tobe never understood why his space made him feel psychologically displaced, and he hated spending time, much less sleeping, in it.

Tobe closed his eyes. He was now panicked enough to take extreme measures: he decided to pray to God for help but was not sure how to begin. Shutting his eyes for a few moments didn't help, so he decided to get down on his knees to see if that would make a difference—and did just that. He thought about the fact that it was the second time that day that he had resorted to his knees to pray. The carpet in his room was much softer than the floor in the preacher's study.

He was now on his knees by his bed, his elbows resting on the bedspread, the palms of his hands pressing together in the locked prayer position, and his eyes closed. Everything was in proper order, physically, to pitifully importune God. Mentally, he was nowhere near ready, because, basically, he did not know what to ask for. He figured a request for the church to burn down would not be granted, although secretly that was what he really wanted—or something similar, like an earthquake, a blizzard (what were the chances in May?), a flood (a more likely possibility but remote), a forest fire that would prevent their getting to church, a bombing attack of the United States by its newest enemy, Russia, anything that would cause them to cancel the Sunday-evening worship service. Finally, he decided to be honest with God—and himself.

"Please, God," he began, "I need help. I've gotten myself into a awful mess and don't know how to git outta it. They're gonna baptize me this evenin'"—(as though God did not know that)—"and I ain't got no idea what it's all about, I don't unnerstand what they're sayin', and I feel like such a phoney-baloney. Please help me get out of this. Pul lease, God?"

Tobe waited. There was nothing but silence.

"God? Are you there?"

More silence followed.

"Please, God, say sump'n or gimme a sign that you're listenin'."

Tobe waited in silence again.

"Just one tiny lit'le ole sign is all I ast."

Suddenly a loud and persistent banging rang out, causing Tobe's nervous system to jerk with a reflexive spasm and an expectation that God was present. Tobe opened his eyes, expecting to see God.

"Hey, little brother! I need to come in. Open this door. Hurry up," came the voice from the other side of the door.

Tobe was momentarily mute, and then—"I'm comin', I'm comin'," he called out as he rose from his knees, feeling disappointed and as though there was something badly wrong in his relationship with God, a feeling he had been warring with.

Tobe looked through the frilly curtains and out the bedroom window. His friend Buddy was playing in their fort, which they had made with the expectation that they would help defend America against the invading German Nazi blitzkrieg. By the time Tobe had begun to develop some awareness of the world in which he lived, around the age of eight or nine, the war was entering its apocalyptic final stages, and graphic images from the daily newspapers (his source being the *Charlotte Observer*) and *Life* magazine (that source being obtained freely at the hynotizing newsstands), as well as the dark, ominous voices on the radio, all these enfolded the edgy nation, including its innocent youth, which should not have been infected by such adult behavior. But they were.

With his BB gun in hand, he approached his friend Buddy already in their fort. The "fort" was the name they had given to what was essentially a large hole in the ground, what World War I soldiers called a foxhole, with the excavated dirt piled on one side to form a small buffer for further protection. They had begun digging the hole with the ambition of digging all the way to China, which they had heard was on the other side of the earth, but as their awareness of the war widened, it became their fort, which everyone knew was necessary to have as protection against invading Nazi hordes. It would later become their nuclear bomb shelter.

"Look what I got," Buddy called to the advancing Tobe as he held up a rather large, round object.

"What is that?" Tobe asked as he jumped down into the hole.

"That's a real Nazi German helmet," Buddy answered as he put it on, causing his voice to reverberate as though it was in a deep, metallic hole.

"Wow," said Tobe. "How'd you git that thaing?"

"My uncle brought it back from the war. He got it off a dead German soldier he killed."

"Good for him. One less Nazi to kill us," Tobe said. As long as he had not yet been baptized, he felt he could approve of killing for a worthy cause.

"He gave it to my mother to keep for him. She don't know I brought it outside," Buddy said, his voice still echoing inside of the helmet.

"Can I touch it?" Tobe asked. Doing so gave him an eerie feeling. For years, all the talk about war, and killings, and violence, and slaughter, and pain, and misery was all so far away, but here, right underneath the touch of his hand, was living proof of its existence, and it had abetted the enemy. He felt as though he had the very embodiment of evil in his hand. He wanted to do something violent, but he didn't know what to do. He wanted revenge, he wanted blood, he wanted to give pain, but he could do nothing: Buddy was wearing the helmet.

"I got an idea," Tobe said. "Let's put it over there some'ers and pretend a German soldier is wearin it. Then we'll git in the fort with our BB guns and try to kill him."

"Naw. What if we hit the helmet instead? My mom would kill me," Buddy said.

"It's okay. A BB gun ain't gonna hurt that thaing," Tobe said. "Look what a chance this is. We can pretend we're shooting at something that was shooting at us—killing Americans. We'll be saving the world. We'll be heroes. We'll be like Captain America. We'll pretend that we're helping Captain America win the war. Come on, Buddy."

"If you git me in trouble—"

"We'll put the helmet on the head of a broom and lean it against that tree. Then we'll get in the fort and aim at the broom head underneath the helmet. That'll be fun, give us something to shoot at."

After they found a broom and properly placed it against a big old pine tree, they got in their fort. While peering over the mound on top of their ditch, Tobe continued with his plans. "Let's pretend we're American soldiers and there's this big, bad Nazi comin at us. When I say 'kill,' we start shootin. Okay?"

They both stared at the helmet.

"Shhhh," Tobe whispered, pretending combat. "Look over there. You see that? There's a Nazi soldier coming at us. Stay down. Don't let 'im see us til he gits closer."

Tobe paused.

"Now, kill! Kill! Kill!" Tobe yelled, and they commenced firing until all their BBs were expended.

"There," Tobe said calmly. "Wadn't that fun?" Little did it occur to him that such action would be inappropriate on the day he was to be baptized.

Buddy said nothing but showed his concern for the helmet.

Tobe's mind returned to his Sunday-morning nightmare.

"They're gonna drown me tonight," Tobe said softly.

"What?" Buddy asked.

"They're gonna drown me tonight."

"Who is?"

"These people."

"What people?"

"At the church. They're gonna drown me."

"Whatta you talkin 'bout?" Buddy said.

"I'm supposed to be baptized at church tonite," Tobe explained.

"Oh. Why?"

"I ain't sure. It's just something they do."

"Why you? What'd you do?"

"I ain't done nothin'—except open my big mouth."

"Did you misbehave in church?" Buddy asked.

"No!"

"But they ain't really gonna drown you, are they?"

"It could happen. They're gonna duck me under water. Who knows?"

"I wouldn't wanna be you," Buddy said.

Tobe responded with dour silence, for his mind seethed with fright.

Back in his room, with some time on his hands before departing for his dreaded appointment with water, Tobe picked up a book, sat down in the uncomfortable rocker, and hid his mind from his evening's rendezvous.

"I want you to get out an old pair of dungarees and your blue plaid shirt to take with you," his father said while standing in the doorway of Tobe's bedroom.

"Why?" Tobe asked.

"You want to mess up another pair of your good Sunday clothes?"

"What?"

"You can't be baptized in your good Sunday clothes. You have to take some old clothes with you. You can change in the little boys' room on the second floor," his father patiently explained.

The thought of wet clothing had not crossed Tobe's mind; he was more preoccupied with images of his submerged body, the thought of which had filled him with terror and blocked out all other realities. His father's instructions had inched him into the compelling circle of reality and paralyzed him; his daddy then left him alone with his nightmare.

Tobe closed his book, rose from the rocker, and moved toward his closet. He was already dressed for church; this was a different mission. He tried to locate his dungarees in the closet, but as his hand slid the clothes hangers along the bar, it was trembling so badly that he kept knocking clothes to the floor. Every chore was made increasingly difficult because of his reluctance to perform it, the completion of which would move him ever closer to the climactic moment.

Tobe was not actually afraid of water, for he and his brother often went swimming in the big ole Catawba River, as dangerous as that was, and even more often in a wide, deep creek behind their grandmother's house, where they played with the colored kids they knew from the little municipal golf course where their daddy played golf. The young boys were caddies, and when Tobe and his brother caddied for their daddy, they got to hang out with the other caddies as well. They had a lot of fun with these boys, with whom they played all kinds of water games, but they were not allowed to go to school with them, or church, or a restroom, or share a drinking fountain with them.

No, it was not the fear of water that was causing Tobe so much suffering and anguish. The fear of drowning, which he had told Buddy about out of mere self-pity and sympathy seeking, was an act of psychological replacement for the real causes of his torment. Tobe tried to understand the complexity of the many elements that comprised his pain. But ultimately there was the feeling that he was being forced into something that he was not even sure what it was and that he was not ready for, a feeling of wanting to take a deep breath in order to slow things down, to call a halt to people who were his superiors and had authority over him and whom he could not contradict or subvert. Additionally, he felt that he was engaging in fraud; he was nowhere near experiencing what they were assuming he was experiencing and were imposing on him. Above all, he began to feel that God must be angry with him and that, surely, if God did pay any attention to him, it would be to punish him for defrauding people and God Himself. Deep inside was the dread that God might strike him dead the second he was immersed in water for making a mockery of, to the Baptist, a sacred enterprise.

It was a mid-May Sunday afternoon, the sun was low in the dimming sky, and they were in their old Model A Ford again on their way to where they always went on Sunday evenings—church. Tobe remained silently subdued by his thoughts, observing through the car window the world outside. Their home was several miles outside of town, and they had to take a rather circuitous route to the church, passing through countryside vistas and open spaces, then penetrating the slightly more populated areas on the rim of the town, on into regular city neighborhoods, passing parks and storefronts, and finally arriving at the destination, East Belhaven Baptist Church.

As Tobe peered fearfully and broodingly out of the window, he saw a world that he was not a part of on this stunning evening. Boys and girls his age were riding bicycles in their neighborhoods, skating on the sidewalks, and playing games such as Red Rover, Hide 'n' seek, and tag on the dark green lawns. He noticed a family enjoying a colorfully decorated birthday party on someone's porch and girls jumping rope in the driveway. In the park, a group of boys were playing baseball, and others were engaged in a game of touch football. Oldsters were tossing horseshoes in the sandpits. Couples were holding hands and embracing and kissing, some lying in the grass, some unbelievably close. Toddlers with droopy diapers were negotiating steps, and old folks were bending into their canes toward unknown destinations. On through the city streets Tobe and his family rode, amid the outside laughter and squealing and screaming and loud talking and singing and music and noisy radios (Gene Autry was singing "Have I Told You Lately That I Love You") and barking and blaring horns, and somewhere someone was playing a fiddle. They were the sounds of life in Belhaven. In the air was the scent of a steak roasting on a grill and popcorn and gardenias and roses and the smell of the river and creeks and brooks and trees and mowed grass and sweat and perfume and cotton mills and the earth. *Someday I'll be free from this jailhouse and have myself a real life,* Tobe thought.

The evening was on everyone's skin, moisture in the air and warm languishing sunlight enshrouding everyone, insects hovering to seize their share of life, and, above all, skin on skin. There was energy and activity and vivacity and fun and joy and happiness and delight in life and being alive, and romance and hope and potential. In order to participate, Tobe thought of the copper-haired girl in his Sunday school class, and then he thought of Jane Russell and the tingle of touching himself.

Tobe was envious. He longed to be out there on a magnificent but, to him, somber eventide, maximizing all that life gives only once. He felt like someone being led to his execution, the condemned person longingly eying that from which he is to be taken. It all deepened his depression and resistance. He hated his life and church and church and religion and Bible stories and water and preachers and his parents and everything that had brought him to this place! But most of all, he hated Sunday evenings.

"Please be seated," the choir director said to the congregation after they had finished singing the last hymn and said a prayer. They prayed a lot in the Baptist Church, Tobe noted. The preacher and Tobe left the sanctuary at the beginning of the last hymn to prepare themselves for the dunking that was to follow.

The area over the baptismal pool was framed like a large window with a curtain that parted to reveal, on the back wall over the water, a mural of John the Baptist standing in the Jordan River, one hand raised in the air, the other on Jesus's back as he is preparing to baptize Jesus. It was a depiction of the story as told in the Gospel of Matthew, chapter 3. The picture shows a dove descending from heaven, a shaft of light coming from somewhere above ("the heavens were opened to him"), and from a dark cloud, according to the scripture, comes a voice saying, "This is my beloved son in whom I am well pleased." Tobe's initiation ceremony was framed by this sacred Baptist story.

The preacher began descending the steps on the left side into the pool, cautiously sinking deeper until his feet reached the bottom, at which point the water came just above the minister's waist. Tobe stood at the top of the steps on the right side, awaiting the preacher's signal. The minister turned to the audience and quoted the story as told in the

Gospels of Jesus's example, concluding with "And Jesus, when He was baptized, went up straightway out of the water: and, lo, the heavens were opened unto Him, and He saw the Spirit of God descending like a dove and lighting upon Him," and then the reverend turned to Tobe and beckoned him with a wave of the hand.

Tobe began to slowly descend, now without a quiver of emotion, for he had stopped fighting against it and settled into a calm, or benumbed, resignation. If he had a thought at this point, it was merely that he hoped the copper-headed girl was watching. Being shorter than the preacher, Tobe was in the water up to his armpits, moving tentatively toward the preacher.

Still facing the audience, the minister whispered to Tobe, "Turn around." Tobe turned sideways to the audience. "Cross your arms over your chest." Tobe did. The minister placed his right hand on Tobe's back, just below his neck, and held in his left hand a folded handkerchief. He began, "In the name of the Father, the Son, and the Holy Ghost," and then placed the handkerchief over Tobe's nose and pushed Tobe backward.

Tobe reacted to the sensation of being pushed under the water and not having control by flailing his arms wildly about. Out of sheer desperation, he began groping for something to hold on to and by chance grabbed his arm around the minister's neck, pulling him downward as Tobe tried to pull himself up. Caught off guard, the minister lost his balance. Then his foot slipped, and the minister went under the water as well.

Everyone gasped while the two in the pool disappeared. Two deacons in the front row ran up on the pulpit and toward the baptismal pool in order to pull them both up, but the minister and Tobe bobbed up on their own. Tobe had swallowed water and was hacking and trying to clear his windpipe while the minister said, "Amen," water streaking down his face. The minister's suit was heavy with water, which caused his movements to be slow and mechanical—*Like Frankenstein,* Tobe thought.

Tobe looked up at Reverend Hicks's wet bald head and crooked glasses and muttered to himself, "Asshole."

In the Model A Ford again, the family sat for a while in silence, until the mother said, "I ain't never been so humiliated in all my life. I can just imagine what Maude Smith is gonna be tellin' the customers in her store t'morrow."

"Yeah," the father agreed and then looked in the rearview mirror at Tobe. "You got anythaing to say?"

"No, sir," Tobe said.

"You can't do anythaing right, can you?"

"I guess not," Tobe mumbled.

"When you get home, I want you to take a shower before you go to bed," his daddy continued. "That water in the baptistery prob'ly ain't too clean."

As though I ain't had enough water for one day, Tobe thought.

The most startling thing happened on that May evening: what had been one of the worst days of his life became one of the best days of his life, a rebirth, so to speak. In the shower, Tobe began to lather his body, cleaning his armpits, his neck, his feet, and then between his legs, which created an extremely gratifying sensation. The image of Jane Russell had now replaced the copper-haired girl in his mind.

It felt like a tingling, warm liquid pulsing through his penis, and his penis began to stiffen and grow. There seemed to be an irresistible force driving the sensations in his body, and he grasped his penis in his hand and began to slowly run his hand up and down the shaft. He had, of course, done this before, but this was something new and beyond ordinary occurrences. There was a compulsion driving his whole body, and his hand began to move faster and faster up and down his penis. Something would not let him stop, would not release him, and he was caught in the power of a force that would not be denied, the impulse of the universe.

He thought about stopping, that he'd had enough, but he could not stop as the pleasant sensation became stronger and stronger, driving, throbbing, sending out waves of the pleasantest sensation he had ever felt, faster and faster, when suddenly there began to stir somewhere deep inside of him something he had never felt in his short lifetime, and then his whole body began to quiver and shiver and shake until it took over his whole being and creamy liquid began to shoot from his penis, and more spasms rocked his whole body until it began to subside, and he was left with the most wonderful peace he had ever known, the pleasantest feeling he had ever felt. He then realized that he had just had his first climax, something he wanted to repeat over and over again. He decided he would do so every day for the rest of his life.

In bed, in the dark, he could not stop thinking about what he had experienced in the shower, and the awful events of the day, including the fiasco of the baptism, faded from his mind, replaced by something far more wonderful. As he was losing consciousness, he remembered that the story in the book of Matthew of Jesus's baptism was followed by Jesus's sojourn into the mountains for forty days and nights where the devil came to Him and tried to tempt Him. But Jesus was strong and said, "Get thee hence, Satan: for it is written, thou shalt worship the Lord thy God, and Him only shalt thou serve."

Funny, Tobe thought as he was falling asleep, *Jesus's baptism was followed by the devil's temptation, as was mine.* His thoughts were suspended for a moment, and then came the completion of the thought before falling asleep. *I don't think I'm as strong as Jesus.* He felt a falling sensation as sleep began overtaking him, and his last thought was, *Maybe Satan ain't so bad after all.*

CHAPTER 2

Belhaven and Mount Berry, Late Summer, 1950

"Daddy?" Tobe was reluctant to ask his father any questions ever since he asked the question about what it meant to be saved, but it was now three years later, he was fifteen, and the year was 1950, the year that commemorated the awareness of an increasingly restive and disgruntled colored population, which would not be patient much longer, and began the march down the corridors to the civil rights movement and into history. Tobe had no one else to rely on when he was curious about something, his brother having joined the navy and departed.

"Yes, son?" His father stood in front of the living room mirror that was over the fireplace, preening and examining himself.

"What does 'alienation of affection' mean?" Tobe sounded guilelessly juvenile.

"Where'd you hear that?" The father turned from the mirror with a stern, quizzical look on his face, he too sounding innocent of any knowledge of what his son was talking about. Everyone in the family knew, but no one discussed it.

"I don't know," he softly replied, wishing he had not asked anything, again.

"C'mon, you had to hear it some'ers." His father was now combing his hair. "Where was it?"

"Well, at school."

"*Where* at school?" His father showed his teeth to the mirror and tried to suck something from them.

"I dunno—nowhere in particular. I jest heard people talkin' around the school." Tobe tried to be as vague as possible without implicating anyone.

"I guess the word is out now," his father said to himself.

"So what does it mean?" Tobe found the phrase attractive and seemingly sexual, a subject very much on Tobe's teenage mind as of late.

"It means stealing somebody else's wife," he said, also being as vague as possible.

"Did Uncle Harold steal somebody's wife?"

"Her husband thainks so," replied his father.

"Is Uncle Harold goin' to jail?"

"Is that what you heard?" His father sat down on the living room Duncan Fife couch.

Tobe sat down in the colonial rocker across from his father, with the Duncan Fife coffee table between them. "I heard he was being sued, that he's being tooken to court by the husband."

"Lord, Lord." The father sighed. "I guess it's all over the county."

"I heard Uncle Harold has a lot of women besides Aunt Ethel," Tobe said.

"I ain't my brother's keeper," the father said, distancing himself.

"Lucky guy," muttered Tobe, who was masturbating his way through his middle teen years and envied his uncle.

"What? Now look here. I don't want you gittin any idears. What my brother is doin' is wrong. The Stanhope brothers have a bad enough reputation with womin as it is. When you're tempted, you git down on your knees and ast God to give you strength."

"Is that what *you* do?"

The father paused. Tobe stared at his father and thought about his father's questionable behavior with women on several occasions.

"Yes." His father closed the discussion.

It was early fall in North Carolina, and the air crackled with it, bracing, obnoxiously colorful, and insidiously subversive. Tobe was in his sophomore year in high school. He had passed through puberty unscathed, almost, and buffered his family's religious fanaticism with activities that made him popular with his classmates: football, glee club, social clubs, dating (such as it was, being carless), school dances (which his parents frowned on), the drive-in movies, and all manner of small-town activities.

Tobe had decided in the summer to try out for football and discovered he had some athletic ability. Because of his size (being fairly well built for a boy his age), he was placed at the fullback position. He discovered he was the second-fastest runner on the team (behind the tailback) and survived the agony of two-a-day August practices. His most memorable moment came when Belhaven was scrimmaging a team from a smaller town. After the varsity had finished its turn, the B team was given a chance, and on the first play, Tobe broke through the line, cut back hard to his right, and discovered an open field all the way to the goal line some seventy years away. He was showing promise and loved the thrill of carrying the ball. He was hooked. Since he was only a sophomore, he did not enter into a lot of games except when Belhaven got a huge lead, but it was sufficient to give him some notice around the school halls. He knew that in a small town like Belhaven, in the South, football players drew lots of attention and respect. He liked the feeling.

Tobe was intelligent enough to make good grades without much effort, thanks in part to his habit of reading. He had grown into a refreshingly handsome and humble (a product of his Christian upbringing) young man, liked by the girls, he noticed, and buddied by the guys, a neat dresser (thanks to his parents), with an open and fetching smile, warmly sociable and gregarious, considerate, polite, and easy to be with. He had a good feeling about himself and his place in the universe as a fifteen-year-old and, to his dismay, remained a virgin.

Several days after the father-son talk about Tobe's uncle Harold's legal troubles, Uncle Harold appeared at their home to deliver kerosene, with a chilly October threatening their comfort while winter was gathering its forces for the attack.

"How much do I owe you?" Tobe's dad asked his brother Harold after Harold had finished pumping a tankful of kerosene into their storage tank. Tobe, sitting in the driver's seat of his uncle's truck (always practicing his driving), was hoping to hear more details about his uncle's philandering and so pretended not to be listening.

Tobe's house was heated by kerosene stoves, as were most people's, and Harold's business was delivering kerosene in his little tanker truck (a converted pickup) to people around the small towns and countryside of Gaston County in Piedmont, North Carolina.

"Six dollars and twenty-five cents," Harold answered.

"Whew! Things are getting so expensive," his brother said.

"I put twenty-five gallons in your tank at twenty-five cents a gallon. That's a bargain. Everythaing's goin up."

"Is that what you charge everybody?" Tobe's dad, Winston, asked. His quizzical eyebrow signaled that he was thinking Harold must have been doing pretty well with his kerosene-delivery business.

"Well ..." Harold paused.

"What?" Tobe's dad turned to look at Harold.

"There are a coupla ladies—" He stopped. "Let's just say I've got a special business deal with a coupla ladies on my rout'."

"You rascal. You oughta be ashamed of yourself." Winston's tone seemed to indicate that he was aware Tobe might be listening.

"Why?" Harold said.

"What about Ethel?"

Tobe thought about his aunt Ethel, Uncle Harold's wife, a poor, homely, long-suffering creature whose husband, Tobe had heard, had been unfaithful to her throughout their marriage. Tobe, from early years being an inquisitive and alert young lad, learned a lot by eavesdropping. In fact, Tobe had heard his uncle firsthand telling stories of how his wife had chauffeured him around with some lady (a different one every Saturday night) he had picked up at the square dance in the town of Maiden, North Carolina (many of whom were no longer maidens after the dance) while Harold and the lady friend would engage in a variety of activities in the back seat. In fact, Tobe had seen his uncle flirting with his own mother. Tobe concluded that he was in fact a rascal, but Tobe, being a sexually obsessed tenth grader, engaged in silent envy of his uncle. He continued pretending to drive with mouth-motor noises, albeit not so loud that he couldn't hear their conversation.

"What about her?" Uncle Harold said. Tobe had learned early on that his uncle enjoyed playing the innocent party and played it well.

"She's your wife," Winston said.

"So, are you telling me that you ain't engaged in a little hanky-panky here and there?" Through the side-view mirror, Tobe saw his uncle smile slyly like a rogue.

"Of course not. I'm a leader in my church. I'm the president of the Gaston County Baptist Association. I'm looked up to and admired all over the county, in Baptist circles. I go to church at least five times a week. I have daily devotionals. I try to obey God."

"Whatta you tryin to prove, Winston?"

"I'm just tryin' to serve my Lord."

"Your way is different from mine."

"Are you sure you're saved?" Tobe's father said.

"Of course I am. I just don't have to try to prove it twenty-four hours a day." Tobe, still observing the conversation from inside the cab, could not help but wonder what it would be like if his uncle Harold was his father instead of his own religiously obsessed father. *Freedom,* he thought.

Tobe exited the truck, and the three of them were now standing in his parents' backyard, close to the kerosene storage tank that Harold had just finished filling and collecting money for.

"Maybe not, but look where it's gotten you," Tobe's dad said.

"What?"

"You know what I'm talking about." His dad was being guarded because of Tobe's presence.

"How would I know what you've got on your mind?"

"The lawsuit?"

"I ain't worried about it." Uncle Harold, for all his mischievousness and devilment, had a knack for acting like the most blameless person possible, maybe, Tobe thought, because he practiced it so much.

"We'll see what the judge has to say about it," his dad said.

"It ain't my fault Hyman Hall can't hold onto his woman." Tobe knew that Hyman Hall was the aggrieved husband of Harold's mistress Pearl.

"Poor Ethel," Tobe's dad said.

"Hey, Tobe, how'd you like to go to Maiden Saturday night?" his uncle said as he turned to Tobe.

"I don't square-dance all that good," Tobe said, avoiding the question.

"Ah, hell, it ain't about square dancin'. It's about all the women they got there—a lot of them your age, and good-lookin' too," his uncle continued.

"I'd love to, but—" Tobe nodded his head toward his father without saying anything more.

"I can fix you up," Uncle Harold said as he grinned lasciviously.

"Don't even think about it," Tobe's father said.

"We'll git around him one of these days." Harold bobbed his head sideways toward his brother.

Tobe wished more than anything he could go with his uncle to one of the dances and do what his uncle did in the back seat of a car.

"He's goin' to a Cottage Prayer meetin' Saturday night," Tobe's father said.

Tobe, without a choice, acceded to his father.

It was the Sunday morning after his uncle Harold filled their kerosene tank on Friday. Tobe's family now had a 1948 Chevrolet Fleetline four-door sedan, and, before most family outings, church or whatever, Tobe liked to arrive at the car first so that he could sit in the driver's seat for a brief moment and practice clutching and shifting (the gear shift being on the steering column behind the steering wheel), reading the instrument panel, looking in the rear and side-view mirrors, tapping the brakes—and pretending to be driving a delicious-looking, high-breasted young lady to the drive-in for an evening of heavy petting, or maybe even more if he got lucky. As a mid-teen boy, he had a one-dimensional mind, and this obsession had pretty much taken over his life, whether it was eating, sleeping (especially sleeping and wet dreams), studying, hanging out with his buddies (the singular topic of conversation), practicing football (his raison d'être for playing football), learning how to drive a car, from a back seat, and, of course, masturbating (how many times a day he masturbated he could not begin to count). He had a keenly sharpened imagination when it came to male/female attractions.

As he was planted in the driver's seat on this Sunday morning, church being the intended destination, of course, and wearing a coat and tie, he practiced looking around for traffic, out the windows, in the mirrors, through the windshield, scanning everything as his father had taught him. His eye caught something on the floor mat in front of the passenger's seat (which seemed odd since his father allowed no trash in his meticulously clean car). He gave it a second look, attempting to decipher exactly what he was looking at. It was a dark object, possibly maroon.

He looked out the passenger-side window to clear his vision and refocus and then brought his eyes back to the floor again. He still was unable to identify something that seemed nothing more than a small, amorphous mass. Finally he decided to act and reached his hand all the way to the floor. He touched it once but could not get his fingers around it, realizing at that point that it was some type of fabric. He then stretched his body and arm even farther, this time successfully snagging the object and pulling himself into the upright position.

Huh, he thought, *it's only a pair of gloves. I guess Mother dropped 'em without realizin it.* Tobe knew that his mother had an extensive collection of lady's dress gloves for church and other dress-up occasions, such as weddings and funerals. He placed them on the seat beside him and returned to his fantasy of driving a young lady to some predetermined destination for lewd purposes.

When he saw his parents approaching on the sidewalk from the house, he opened the driver's-side door, picked up the gloves, and proceeded around to the front of the car to meet his parents at the end of the sidewalk.

Coming around to the passenger side of the car, Tobe said, "So, Mother, have you lost anything lately?"

She raised her hand immediately to her right ear as if to reassure herself that her earring was still there, which it was, and answered, "No, I don't think so." Tobe's dad stopped in front of the car as he was crossing to the driver's side and turned to look back out of curiosity.

"Are you sure?" Tobe continued with his game.

"Stop your silliness, Tobe. Whatta you talkin' about?" his mom said as she started to open the passenger door.

"How about these?" Tobe lifted the gloves up in front of her, which she cautiously took from his hand, examining them closely and silently for a brief moment. His father still stood at the front of the car with a blank face.

"These ain't mine," she said.

"Whatta you mean?" Tobe asked. "Of course they're yourn."

"Where'd you get these?" she asked.

"They were on the floor of the car, in front of the passenger seat. I thought they were yourn."

"Well, they ain't. I've never owned a pair of gloves like this in my life."

"Are you sure?" Tobe was puzzled.

"You think I don't know what I own and what I don't?" She then looked at her husband and said, "Winston?"

"Don't look at me. They ain't mine," he answered.

"Whose gloves are these?" she asked, holding them up and shaking them.

"I said don't look at me." The father suddenly blanched, looking like the personification of panic.

"You're the only one that's been in the car."

"I don't know nuthin 'bout them."

"Tobe," his mother said, turning to him again, "since when did you start wearin lady's gloves?"

"C'mon, Mother, I don't know nuthin' bout 'em."

"Winston?" She turned to her husband again.

"Git in the car. We're gonna be late." The father continued around to the driver's door, which he opened and got in.

In the car, silence ruled briefly. Tobe, in the back seat, noted his father's eyes in the rearview mirror, eyes like he had never seen on him before. They looked like they were going to pop out of their sockets. His mother was breathing loudly, as though preparing for the long jump or for battle. Tobe wondered if indeed his father did take after his older brother Harold after all.

"Okay, let's go over this again," his mother began. "I know for a fact that these gloves ain't mine, the odds of their being Tobe's is remote, and the gloves did not just magically appear on the floor of the car. They got there somehow, put there by somebody. That leaves only one person who knows how those gloves got there, and that's you, Winston. So, either you bought them for yourself, which seems pretty silly, unless you've started a new lifestyle, or you bought them for someone else and accidentally dropped them, or the third possibility is that someone seated in this seat was carryin 'em and accidentally dropped them."

Tobe was impressed with his mother's analytical skills and logic, which he had never seen before. It was her finest moment, in Tobe's eyes at least. But he was not sure whose side he was on. He looked at his father from the back seat, and a drop of sweat was sliding down the back of his neck. He sensed that his father was trapped.

"These dang pokey drivers. Hurry up, buddy. We runnin late here!" His father clearly wished they were already at their destination—his sanctuary, church.

"Never mind the traffic. We're not gittin outta this car until we git to the bottom of this." Tobe had never seen his mother so persistent.

Silence dangled in the air like a loose rope with which his father was about to hang himself.

"I'm waitin'," she said as she, from Tobe's perspective, tightened the noose.

"Okay. I'm gonna tell you the God's truth." Tobe wondered if his father had finally come up with a story or if they were about to hear the real truth. "Remember t'other day when I had to go to Cha'lotte and it was pourin rain?"

"Yes." It was the iciest yes Tobe had ever heard.

"I was on the Wilkerson Boulevard—just where the city limits sign is—goin' into Cha'lotte—there's a bus stop there. Know where I'm talkin' about?"

"Yes," she snapped.

"Well, I seen this poor woman tryin' to stay dry with her umbrella open, so I stopped and asked her if she wanted a ride, and she said sure and opened the door. She must have dropped the gloves when she got in the car. That's all there was to—"

"Where'd you take her?" Tobe's mother said.

"I dropped her off downtown—on the square to be exact, corner of Trade and Tryon." The father exhaled, seemingly relieved.

"What'd you talk about?" his mother asked.

"Nuthin. The weather. This 'n' that."

"You git her name?"

"Uhhh—no, as a matter of fact, I didn't."

Tobe wondered about the hesitation in his father's voice while the father looked in the rearview mirror at Tobe, who saw lies in his eyes.

The Stanhope family car pulled into a parking space in the street next to the church, and just as the mother was touching the door handle, the daddy said, "Wait." Time stopped.

"Let's say a prayer before we go inside." Tobe was used to this, his usual ploy. "Dear heavenly Father, we thank Thee for this glorious Sunday mornin and for the beautiful family here present. We come to Thee in all humility to ask Thy forgiveness for any wrongdoings we have committed. We know that You, God, are a forgivin' God and will forgive us our sins if we just ast, which we now do. Now bless this family in our love for You and for each other. In Jesus's name we pray. Amen. Let's go inside and forget all that's happened. Everything is right with God now."

Mother exited from her side of the car while Tobe pulled the handle on the back door on the driver's side. Just as he was pushing the door open, he was startled by the power of the grip on his right arm from the front seat. His father fumed at him, gritting his teeth, and hoarsely whispered, "Don't you ever do anything like that agen." It was the ugliest hiss Tobe had ever heard.

"What?" Tobe murmured.

"If you ever find anything like that agen, the last thaing you do is show it to your mama." He exited the car.

"Good mornin," his father said cheerily to a couple of church members standing on the sidewalk. "God has given us another one of His beautiful mornin's. Praise be to God." The mother lovingly and affectionately took her husband's arm as they turned toward the church.

Tobe stood on the sidewalk and pondered what had just happened and thought, *Does his warnin me to never do it agen mean that he plans to keep on doin whatever it is he's doing?* Tobe turned in the direction of the church library, which was in a little house separate from the main church, to ferret out some more *Hardy Boys* adventures. There he met his friend Jack, Jack Workman, the preacher's son, who was looking for anything on cars, his teenage passion.

The excessive religious exposure resulted in one positive benefit in Tobe's barren life. East Belhaven Baptist Church acquired a new minister when Tobe was in eighth grade, Reverend Hicks having retired, and the new minister, Reverend Workman, had a young family that included a boy Tobe's age named Jack. On Jack's first day at Tobe's school, Tobe, who was a student worker in the principal's office, met Jack, gave him a tour of the campus (at the principal's request), and then showed him to his homeroom. They were both in eighth grade and became instant friends. Tobe and Jack discovered that they had similar temperaments and an excessive interest in girls. Like all pubescent guys, they suffered from constant horniness, which remained unrequited till later years.

"Hey, Tobe," Jack greeted him, looking up from the latest car magazine (the congregation donated any number of books and publications to the church library when cleaning out their junk—and to write off their income tax).

"Jack," Tobe replied, holding several books.

"Listen, I've got Dad's car this afternoon. Wanna see if we can drag main, maybe over in Mount Berry and in Gastonia?" Jack asked.

"You bet."

"We'll talk about it after church," Jack said as he checked out from the library the magazine he was holding.

Inside the church stood Winston Stanhope, who served in the capacity, among other positions, as superintendent of Sunday school, no insignificant position, overseeing the whole operation, from the tiniest kindergarten classes to the eldest senior citizen study groups, and all ages and genders in between. It was, next to being chair of the board of deacons (which he also was), the most prestigious lay position in the church.

"Good morning, ladies and gentlemen and my fellow believers in Christ," Stanhope began. "Let's begin our program this morning with a prayer. Oscar, would you lead off with our first prayer this morning?"

So Oscar Oswald began, and he prayed and he prayed and he prayed and he prayed some more, a long, rambling petition to God, telling God everything that Oscar thought God would want to hear. In the Southern Baptist Church, there is a fierce competition to see who can pray the loudest and the longest, to see who can be the most righteous, the most sanctimonious as displayed through the art of orisons. By the time Oswald finished his prayer, Stanhope said, "Let's go to our respective classes now." Tobe thought his father sounded disappointed because he had been deprived of his turn to pray, and then Tobe snickered as he thought of Oscar Oswald's Olympic Orisons.

Mount Berry, Early Fall, Court Room, 1950

When Harold Stanhope's trial began, it was several weeks later that same fall, and Hyman Hall was suing Harold Stanhope with the charge of "alienation of affection" because Harold was having an affair with Hyman's wife, Pearl. Tobe had heard all the rumors and speculation. What did Hyman expect to receive for his effort? To get his wife's affection returned to him? To make a dent in Harold's bank account, as meager as it was? To restore order to his family of two daughters, to, perhaps set an example for them? To protect his own sense of dignity? To express his anger? To achieve justice? To punish his wife and Harold? Tobe arrived at the realization that no one knew what lay in the murky depths of the primitive vestiges (one ape protecting his territory from another ape?) in Hyman's mind, but as Tobe interpreted it, the only thing he accomplished, which may have been his real motivation, was a total and complete embarrassment of the Stanhope family, except for one member of the family: Tobe wondered if his uncle's reputation might add a little luster to his own reputation as a "lady's man."

Through the fall months of 1950, Tobe heard the "word" everywhere he turned, the barbershops, the breakfast counters in the drugstores, the lunch counters in the diners, the dinner tables in the restaurants, the shop counters in the local five-and-dime, the sales tables in department stores large and small, in the beauty parlors (he overheard his mother mentioning this), and even in the sanctuaries and halls of the churches. There was nowhere he could present himself without hearing gossip about "The Trial." Tobe heard questions like: How could someone put himself through such public humiliation? What kind of evidence will be offered up? What kind of stories will be told? Who can serve as witness to such a suit? What, beyond hearsay, could be established? Will the offenders be called as witnesses to testify against each other? The whole county was rife with speculation, false gossip, flimsy rumors, tongue clucking, moral indignation, condescension, feelings of superiority, and ethical judgments, and every conceivable opinion, lie, and fact was being circulated. At least that was Tobe's perspective.

Harold Stanhope had four brothers—Floyd (the oldest), Winston (who came next after Harold), Fred the would-be theologian, and the youngest, Earl—and three sisters—Vera, the oldest, Gladys, the next in line, and Grace, who had a baby girl born out of wedlock. The brothers and sisters were gravely concerned about what was happening with their brother Harold and decided to conduct a meeting to determine the proper course of defensive action for the family. Floyd, who lived a considerable distance in another town, phoned in his regrets because he was on the road with his truck driving.

It was in the old family home where the meeting of the siblings took place, in the musty, dark living room with a small autumn fire in the fireplace, and where Tobe's grandmother had lain in state. Tobe and some cousins were sitting on the front porch just outside the living room window, listening intently. Tobe was particularly interested in the activities of his notorious uncle.

Gladys and Grace also still lived in the old family home where Tobe's grandmother had died and where he, when younger, went swimming in the creek behind the house. They kept chickens, pigs, a cow, and a vegetable garden to bolster their subsistence. The house had no running water (except for a hand-pumped faucet on the back porch), which necessitated "slop jars" under the bed at nighttime, no electricity, which necessitated kerosene lamps throughout the house, and no washing facilities, which necessitated washing clothes (religiously every Monday) in a wash pot, a large cast-iron vat in the side yard (near the smoke house), which was heated by a wood-kindling fire. Tobe always remembered the washboard that they used and the nonelectric irons that were heated in front of the fireplace.

"I jest want to say," Gladys began, "that Harold's our brother, and we need to show him our support." Tobe's favorite of all his uncles and aunts was the matriarch-type figure in the family, the second-oldest sister, Gladys, who held her respected position by virtue of her loving, giving, kind, motherly nature, so interested in all the nieces and nephews as though they were her own flesh and blood. She lived her life as a spinster, except for a six-month marriage, and was addicted to snuff, which she always had a dip of between her lower lip and her lower front gum. She was constantly covering her mouth with her hand and apologizing for her nasty habit (Tobe saw her live to the age of ninety-four).

"Support his messing around with a married woman," Tobe's dad said. Tobe's admiration for his father increased during Tobe's middle-teen year as his father became more self-sufficient. His father had recently bought some large acreage and given up his mill job; he developed a fishing lake, which was rather profitable, was building a fish camp (a North Carolina phenomenon of homey restaurants specializing in fried fish), was parceling off land tracks for houses, and was becoming an independent businessman.

"Watch it now," Harold said.

"I think we should all be present and sit in the front row of the courtroom and let everybody know how we feel about our brother," Gladys continued.

"I can't take the time off. I've got beer to deliver," Earl said.

The youngest brother was Earl, who drove a beer truck, held an enormous stash of beer and liquor in his garage, and teetered on the brink of being an alcoholic. They all had a fairly grim outlook on life due to the strict and severe puritanical nature of their upbringing, but some, such as Earl the comic, were determined to fight in any feeble way they could the gloom that threatened all their haunted psyches. Tobe was charmed and intrigued by his uncle Earl's sense of humor.

"People can go a day without beer," Winston said.

"But I can't go without my paycheck," Earl fired back.

"It ain't necessary, Earl," Harold said. "I'll be aw right."

"I ain't goin'," Fred asserted. Uncle Fred was a rather elephantine, lumbering hulk of a man who, while in his forties, had a nervous breakdown and quit working. He remained all his life a fretful type, had a brilliant and retentive mind, and spent his waking hours reading the Bible and biblical commentaries. His siblings were convinced that God had called him to be a preacher but that he ignored God's summons, which was the basis of his nervous system problems. Tobe was especially interested in his uncle Fred's knowledge of the Bible and theology and often sat to chat with him out of a great eagerness to learn.

"It's no good if we ain't all there," Gladys stated, trying to advocate for family unity and support for her brother.

"I ain't goin'," Fred repeated, folding his arms.

"I'll give you a ride," Winston said.

"I won't git in your car."

"You can't do this, Fred," Gladys said.

"I ain't goin'." Fred stood up, and Tobe wondered if he was threatening to leave.

"Leave 'im alone," Harold said.

"Why cain't you go?" Winston asked.

"I don't ride in cars no more, too dangerous. Besides, crowds make me nervous," Fred explained. Silence fell. Tobe and all the family knew that Fred was so apprehensive that, instead of going to bed at nighttime, he slept in a chair in an upright position, probably in a vain effort to feel in control, Tobe speculated.

"Hey, Fred," Vera said after a moment, "don't worry. I'll have a bottle of whiskey in my purse. We'll step outside ever' one-st in a while and take a swig. That'll keep you calm." Tobe's aunt Vera was the oldest sister, divorced from a man named Luke, and the mother of three. She lived in poverty and inertia, tended also toward alcoholism, and had a son, JT, who was a dedicated alcoholic (a thread of alcoholism ran through the family genes in spite of, or perhaps because of, all their efforts at religion). Tobe had once personally witnessed her son's abuse of her when JT, both being tipsy, tried to open a closet door and knocked her down. It left an ugly scar on his memory of his cousin. Tobe felt that his father's family had many skeletons in their individual and collective closets, his aunt Vera's being only one of many.

"I ain't goin'. That's the end of it," Fred concluded.

Gladys turned to her eldest sister. "Vera, are you in?"

"As long as I have my bottle of whiskey with me," Vera said.

"And Grace is comin' with me," Aunt Gladys explained.

"Only's if I can step outside one-st in a while for a smoke," Grace, a dedicated chain smoker, said. Tobe's aunt Grace was the youngest member of the family and had a congenital defect referred to as a hole in the roof of her mouth, so Tobe was told, which gave her speech the unusual sound of speaking into a hollow tube, as Tobe defined it; she was also unable to distinctly clip off each word, causing all words to sort of run together. It was unknown to the brothers who the father of her child was, so Tobe had heard; he concluded that she protected the father's identity to keep her brothers out of her business. She lived under the auspices of sister Gladys, who took the illegitimate child, Gloria (Tobe's cousin), in as her own. Tobe felt great compassion for his aunt Grace, who was only in her mid-twenties.

"So that makes three of us. Fred and Earl and Floyd, of course, are out." She turned to her brother. "Winston, how about you?"

"I jest want everybody to know that I don't like this a little bit," Winston began.

"Save the sermon, Winston. We know how you feel, Mr. Baptist Church," Harold said.

At this point, Tobe's mother, Augusta, who had expressed her feelings at home about the situation, began, "I have never been so humiliated in my whole life. This whole thaing—"

"Why," Harold jumped in, "it ain't no skin off your nose."

"Everywhere I go, the grocery store, the beauty parlor, church, downtown, I can see people talkin' behind my back—snickerin' and whisperin and gossipin' and pointin'—and, and, I'm tellin'you—. We're the laughin' stock. It's jest so upsettin'."

"But we're family," Winston said. "I don't like it, but we'll be there—not as an expression of approval—God knows—but Augusta and me will be sittin' in the front row with Gladys, Grace, and Vera. 'Cause you're our brother. But I still keep thinkin' 'bout Mama and Papa. They must be spinnin' in their graves."

"So that makes five total," Gladys said. "That's better'n nuthin."

"Harold stuck hisself into this situation, so to speak; let him pull himself out of it, so to speak. That's what I say," Fred said, justifying his refusal to attend the trial.

"Well, I jest wanna say that I 'preciate y'all bein' there. It means a lot to me," Harold said, concluding the meeting.

Tobe and his cousins had listened with great interest to all that was said, the window being slightly raised, and now Tobe began to process it, wondering how this was going to affect his standing among his friends and teammates. Among his guy friends, he might well be a hero, but among his female classmates, he might well be a leper. On the other hand, there may well be some girls who were not turned off by the Stanhope reputation and might make themselves available to him; it was a situation to be devoutly wished for. How he dreamt of innumerable and passionate sexual encounters, without ever having had one.

"I think we should have a prayer before we go," Winston suggested. "Fred. Why don't you lead us in prayer."

I knew it, Tobe thought. *My dad has to throw religion in everywhere and pray about everything. It's kinda embarrassing—all this religion stuff.*

"No," Fred responded.

"What?"

"You don't go before the throne of God with frivolous matters. That's a sin," Fred explained. Everyone deferred to Fred in issues of theology.

Tobe's immediate family, living midway between two small towns, Belhaven and Mount Berry, worked, shopped, worshipped, and schooled in Belhaven, while the remainder of the Stanhopes gravitated toward Mount Berry, within whose provenance the old family home stood, as well as Harold Stanhope's residency and kerosene business. Tobe had been instructed in the Stanhope legacy, which stretched a long way back in this little town, which was in their era a dying agrarian economy and being supplanted by textile mills, which was what in the first place had drawn them down from the mountains of North Carolina where they were poor dirt farmers. Thus, when Hyman Hall decided to sue Harold Stanhope for "alienation of affection" from his wife, he took his case to the authorities in Mount Berry, which was a less familiar landscape for Tobe and his family.

Just before the trial began, Tobe's father decided to drive into Mount Berry on the prior weekend to reconnoiter the geographical features, the location of the municipal court, parking areas, and attendant information. While riding down the main street, which was only about three or four blocks long and where the city offices were located, Tobe pointed out to his father that there was a movie house several doors down from the town offices and that *The Grapes of Wrath* was showing, a rerun of the old 1940s black-and-white movie with Henry Fonda. It just so happened that Tobe had been studying Steinbeck's novel, on which the movie was based, in school and was quite eager to see it.

On one Saturday afternoon, Tobe managed to get himself to the downtown area of Mount Berry, mainly by hitching a ride, a perfectly acceptable and safe way, as Tobe perceived it, for a young man to reach his destination, largely because everyone knew everyone—being a hermetically sealed white culture. Since he was a little early for the movie, he decided to drop into the local drugstore for a milkshake and test the atmosphere of this unfamiliar town.

After ordering his butter pecan milkshake at the counter and selecting a booth to slide into, he settled in to enjoy his shake and check out the action, what little there was on a Saturday afternoon. Tobe knew that Sunday afternoons were usually the high-volume time in these small towns ringed around the outskirts of Charlotte, when any teenager with a driver's license and their parents' car for a brief afternoon could go around from small town to small town, all within a few miles of each other, to drag the main street to check out the action. No one really expected anything significant (i.e., romantic) to happen in the context of such activity, although Tobe had been picked up several times by a car full of girls from neighboring towns, especially the county seat, which was the largest town in the county, for a few hours of innocent laughing and joking. Tobe understood that it was all part of the mating ritual for mid-teenagers in this part of the universe.

By contrast, Saturdays were a time for shopping, working, family, movies, sports, and generally catching up. Tobe had a passion for movies on Saturday afternoons, especially in the fall when his body was recovering from the rigor of football practice, viewing several cartoons, the serials, and the main feature, often more than once, usually in Belhaven or East Belhaven near his church but never before this in Mount Berry. Saturdays were for slowing down and taking a break from church.

While Tobe was savoring the first sip of his shake, a voice from behind him asked, "Do I know you?" He turned to look over his left shoulder to see if he was the one being spoken to. He discovered a petit, blonde girl with a pageboy hairdo standing beside his booth. She was very white-skinned with blue eyes, a small chest but a cute figure, a pretty smile, and a square jaw, and was wearing a long skirt, a white blouse, and saddle oxfords.

"Are you talkin' to me?" Tobe said.

"No, I'm talkin' to the wall."

"Oh, that's what I thought."

"My name's Barbara," she said as she passed his table and scooted into the booth seat facing him.

"I'm Tobe," he said. *Pretty cute,* he thought. Tobe was constantly sizing up girls—as well as women, ladies, waitresses, teachers, anyone of the female gender. Such were his hormones.

"Tobe?" she questioned with a quizzical look on her face and a tilted head.

"Tobe," he affirmed. He suddenly saw what a ridiculous name it was.

"What's that short for?"

"Short for nothing. That's my name—Tobe." *Why did my parents do this to me?* he wondered.

"Where you from, Tobe?" He liked the sound of her voice and the look of her mouth, which he stared at as she spoke.

"River Heights," he said, "but I go to school in Belhaven."

"Country boy, huh?" River Heights was a neighborhood outside of the city limits of both Belhaven and Mount Berry and in between the two towns; at one point, it had been farmland and tillage but was no longer so. Tobe assured her he was not a country boy.

"So what are you doin' in Mount Berry today?" she asked.

"Actually, I've come to see a movie."

"Which one?"

"The Grapes of Wrath."

"I don't believe it!" she said.

"Why?"

"That's where I'm goin'." Tobe wondered if she was fibbing.

"Are you making this up?" He figured honesty was the best way to impress her.

"Two o'clock show?" she said, guessing correctly.

"Bingo."

"Let's go together," she suggested.

This caused a tingle in Tobe's nether region. She was, after all, an attractive young lady and, as he saw it, his first foray into foreign soil in Mount Berry. He had long ago concluded that the girls in his high school in Belhaven were the homeliest creatures in the universe, all good sisterly friends of his.

"Sure, why not," Tobe agreed, "but I ain't got enough to pay for both our ways in," which was after all only seventy-five cents, pretty pricey for his limited budget, earned primarily by cutting his father's grass. In his early teen years, he had a paper route and saved his money, but once he started playing football, he had to relinquish the newspaper-delivery service.

So Tobe lived, yet again, with a bag of popcorn in his hand on a Saturday afternoon, like so many Saturdays, in a joyless, limited environment through the odyssey and outrage of the Joads. He watched the Joads in their migration from Oklahoma to California and all the misfortunes they endured before, during, and after their sojourn: he observed their poverty, hardship, adversity, struggles, bad luck, injustices, oppression, hard labor, and exploitation. Tobe related to the Joads on a deeply personal, visceral level, although he could not describe it verbally, for, like his own family, the Joads were poor, simple, and plain but well-meaning, goodhearted, kind people with whom life had not been gentle. He thought about his father's family who migrated out of the mountains of North Carolina, without two pennies to rub together, in search of a better life, knowing nothing but poverty, hard-scrabble, unproductive, back-breaking dirt farming, and a meager existence with little to eat, little to wear, and little to look forward to.

And then he thought about his mother's family's history, which most closely resembled the Joads'—

"Tobe?" His thoughts were interrupted by a whisper out of the darkness next to him. He leaned his head toward the voice. "You're awfully cute," she said.

"So are you," Tobe replied, and then came a loud "Sssshhhh!" from behind them.

Barbara then moved her hand over to touch Tobe, who responded by taking her hand, and so they sat through the remainder of the Joad agony, holding hands, which excited Tobe immensely. He liked the feel of the warmth of her body and the smoothness of her youthful skin. Something awakened within him, something strange and wonderful and compelling and irresistible. He decided, as after his first climax, that he would give free play to such feelings for the rest of his life.

"Tobe, you want to walk me home?" Barbara asked as they exited the Mount Berry movie house amongst a small matinee crowd.

"Where do you live?"

"I live here in town—just three or four blocks that way," she answered, pointing in the direction away from the movie house and past town hall.

"Sure," Tobe said.

It was a blessed late-October afternoon, Tobe's favorite time of the year, the month of his birth. The trees were stunning and swathed in autumn colors, as was Tobe. The chrysanthemums blotched the fall gardens with every available color, and the slanting sun projected a magic sheen over the whole picture. He was so moved by the moment and his residual empathy for the Joad family that he knew he would never forget it. Something was definitely happening to him. He felt wistful, pensive, philosophical, if a fifteen-year-old can be that steadily focused without glandular interference. And it was beyond that, for the moment. They were just passing the city hall building where his uncle Harold's trial was to be held. Tobe squashed the thought as soon as it arose.

"Cat got your tongue?" Barbara lifted her eyes up to him. Tobe noticed her petite size and thought of attendant bodily attributes. He remained mentally paused for a moment and then launched himself into the present place and time.

"Do you know what the title of *The Grapes of Wrath* means?" Tobe asked as he moved to the next subject of his attention.

"It's a funny title, don't you think?" she said.

"Not really. Do you know the 'Battle Hymn of the Republic'?"

"Sort of," she said.

"Mine eyes have seen the glory, blab, blab, blab, blab, blab, blab, blab," he said singingly.

"We're Rebs; we don't sing that song," she said.

Tobe continued singing the tune. "He is trampling out the vintage where *the grapes of wrath* are stored."

"Oh."

"See?" Tobe was pleased with himself. He had already begun to sound pontifical at an early age.

"But what does that mean?" Barbara asked.

"Well, what does wrath mean?"

"Wrath, like the wrath of God?"

"Exactly."

They turned up the street that Barbara lived on, a tree-covered lane, quiet, homey, humble, the sanctuary of millions of Americans in those halcyon days.

"Tobe. You're so smart."

"Not really," he said. "We studied it in class. As well as the Civil War."

"I'm not a very good student," she shyly admitted.

"The song is set in the Civil War—where there's lots of anger between the North and the South—they're mad at each other, what with all the fightin—that's the wrath. And the song says that God is gonna trample the anger—the grapes of wrath."

"Wow, Tobe."

"Like I said, we studied it in school."

"But what does that have to do with the movie?"

"Well, that's the tricky part, but my opinion is, after all that happens to the Joads, they have a right to be mad—but they ain't."

"I find the movie to be very depressin," Barbara admitted.

"Well, yeah, but there's one thing." Tobe paused. He was unsure as to whether to go on, not wishing to sound too much like a smartass.

"What's that?"

"You'll notice—after all this crap that happens to the Joads, all the poop they're goin' through—they never complain. They just keep on pluggin' away—just tryin' to survive—never quittin'." Tobe mumbled, "That movie always gets to me." He then changed the subject. "What'd you think of the last scene?"

"Where she's breastfeedin' that old man? I thought it was weird." She shuddered.

"That's not the point. It's a sign of hope and that there's still some goodness in the world, in spite of everything that's happened."

"Wow, Tobe, I'm impressed," Barbara said. "This is my house here." She pointed to the house they were standing in front of.

"This one? Nice."

"You wanna sit on the front porch for a little bit?" Barbara asked.

"I gotta go purty soon. See if I can catch a ride. But sure, just for a minute," Tobe agreed.

"The movie was depressin—but very—uh, I don't know—interestin'?" Barbara said after they were seated on the porch swing.

"Yeah, I relate to that story in a very personal way," Tobe said.

"How's that?"

"The same thaing happened to my mother's family."

"Tell me about it," Barbara said.

"My mother came from a long line of successful farmers in southern South Carolina, with lots and lots of land," Tobe began.

"Do they still have the farm?"

"Nope. Lost it all."

"Poor management?"

"Nope. Bad luck." He paused and then launched the family tale. "Here's how it was: every farmer needs lots of sons to help him with the work on the farm. Right? Well, they had lots of children, all right, thirteen of which were girls. That was the first problem. My grandfather had no help and was overworked. Then, like every farmer, he took out a loan at the beginnin' of the season to git the crops in the ground and used the farm as collateral. That summer, he had a stroke and died at the age of forty-five. So what did the bank do?"

"Took the farm?"

"You got it. Fifteen children all told and no one to take over the farm. The two boys were still just kids. Just like what happened with the Joads. The bank repossessed the farm and drove them off the land. God-dang banks!" There was still a lot of angry venom in Tobe's mother's family, which Tobe had inherited through his mother's milk.

"So what'd they do?" Barbara asked.

"What could they do? Scattered like a flock of biddy chicks in a thunderstorm. They had to go lookin for work; some of them, like my mother, came here because of the textile mills, which hires women by the thousands at poverty wages. Some of them went other places, some of them stayed in South Carolina. Everybody had to find work—except for my grandmother—who was too old to find anythaing. All she knew how to do was make babies."

Barbara's silence spoke volumes.

"Can I see you agen?" Tobe asked. The magic was broken, but he knew the sun was quitting and he needed to get a ride and get home.

"I'll never speak to you again if you don't," she said. "What's your last name, Tobe?'

"Stanhope. And yours?"

"Rimes. Rhymes with rhymes." They then exchanged telephone numbers.

Feeble, Tobe thought. Tobe's inclination was toward smart women.

Because football falls were a demanding time of the year for Tobe, with classes, study hall, football practices, football games, and stoking friendships, in addition to his personal chores, his attendance at his uncle's trial, as badly as he wanted to go, seemed unlikely. Toward the end of the week, however, the planets aligned for him. While the trial had been dragging along for several days with legal positioning and posturing, attorney haggling, judge's warnings and delays, witness examining and cross-examining, and constant recesses for consultations, by Thursday the trial seemed to be approaching a terminal point, the very day of the week during football season when the football team was given a day off to rest up for the big game on Friday night.

With the trial still going on, Tobe campaigned his parents to let him take a day off from school and go with them to the trial, a request debated by his parents. His father finally prevailed with the argument that Tobe could learn something from the trial, not only about the legal system and procedures but about "crime and punishment," by observing the consequences of—as his father articulated it, "sin," which he had warned his brother Harold about. Tobe had other ideas about what was to be learned.

Tobe worked his way through the throng, for the courthouse was packed, with lines up the hall, down the stairs, and out the front door. The whole county was deeply curious about this strange trial. Fortunately, Harold's lawyer had reserved special passes for Harold's family with the justification that they might be needed as character witnesses, and Tobe was able to get inside, where he chatted with his aunts a brief moment before the judge appeared and the action commenced. Tobe was keenly alert and was particularly impressed and interested in the legal proceedings and the serious tone of the whole atmosphere.

It seemed to Tobe that the county attorney, Harley Taylor the prosecutor, was having a difficult time keeping a straight face in spite of the seriousness of the occasion, smiling, smirking, and turning his head aside at one point to indulge in a loud laugh, at which point his uncle's attorney, Weeb Moore, tried to establish the frivolous nature of the whole suit, which the judge overruled with the admonition that North Carolina's laws were not without weight and substance. Another thing that Tobe learned was that North Carolina was one of a very few states that had such a statute as "alienation of affection," which the defense attorney also raised in order to discredit the charges. The judge made it clear that they were not there to prosecute North Carolina.

The moment came when Uncle Harold's attorney cross-examined the aggrieved husband, Hyman Hall. Tobe watched closely as Hall took the stand, noting his worn, old but clean clothes, his stooped posture as though he were cowed by life, the somber expression on his face, and the frightened look in his eyes. He was barely audible when he spoke and seemed to have difficulty answering questions and was asked several times to speak louder. Tobe felt genuine compassion for what seemed like a broken human being, beaten, embarrassed, humiliated, and just plain sorrowful. Tobe secretly wished he had not come to the trial, so sad it was and depressing—and not sexy at all, as Tobe had hoped it would be.

Weeb Moore dug into the statutes of the state and established the fact that in order to charge someone with alienation of affection, it has to be proved that there was an affectionate relationship between the husband and wife in the first place, from which she had become alienated. Tobe wondered how one establishes that there was affection. Moore was relentless and finally established, without Tobe remembering all the details, that Pearl and Hyman Hall had not lived together for the last two years. The prosecutor in rebuttal tried to establish that the reason they were not living together was that Tobe's uncle Harold had started an affair with Mrs. Hall a little over two years ago. Tobe thought it was a draw. The judge saw it differently and, being a bench trial, dismissed the case. But the damage to everyone's reputation was firmly established.

Pearl Hall had two daughters, whom Tobe had met previously, one of whom was almost his age and, in Tobe's mind, very hot. It just so happened, because they were also family members at the trial, they were seated right behind Tobe and his family.

When the trial was over, the large crowd exited slowly, which gave Tobe a chance to turn around to say hello to the daughter his age.

"Hello back," Carol Hall said.

"I hope you don't have any bad feelings toward me because of this," Tobe said.

"You ain't done nutin'."

"Are you in the phone directory?"

"Under my mother's name," she said.

"Mind if I give you a call sometime?" Tobe asked.

"Nope."

"Maybe we could have a Coke or sump'n."

"Okay."

Not exactly the talkative kind, Tobe thought as the row she was sitting in started moving out toward the aisle.

"I heard that," Tobe's dad whispered.

"What?"

"Jest don't go gittin any ideas," his father said as Tobe's row started to exit.

But Tobe, being a fifteen-year-old male, was in constant vigilance mode, always looking for something to catch fire with a member of the female population. *She seemed like a possibility,* Tobe thought. *Maybe Uncle Harold can put in a good word for me. It's a thought.*

Later the same evening, Tobe telephoned Barbara to talk about the possibility of seeing her on Saturday, even though he had no car, no money, no transportation, no resources other than his two feet, and nothing to offer her by way of entertainment or amusement, except his mother wit. What he had in mind was a "date," a procedure in which a boy went to a girl's house in a car to take her out for an evening. The ritual consisted of meeting her parents and establishing the fact that he is a "nice" boy with no evil intentions, that he comes from an respectable family, that he goes to church and Sunday school every Sunday, that he is a conscientious student who plans to "make something of himself" in life, that he doesn't drink or smoke (in North Carolina, the land of tobacco farmers and manufacturers, exceptions could be made to the smoking rule), that he is a responsible driver, and that he will have her home by her curfew, which was usually about ten o'clock, late by local standards. It was an extra benefit if the boy played high school football. After visiting with the parents a bearable amount of time and entertaining them with his charm and reassuring them with his niceness, he then takes her out.

None of these events were on Tobe's agenda when he called Barbara for a date, since he had no car and no money. What he had in mind was to go see her on a Saturday night, meet her parents, visit for a while, and then hope that the parents disappeared into a back room somewhere, or perhaps he and Barbara could take a walk, maybe visit one of her girlfriends, visit a nearby park where they might hold hands, do a little hugging, and, with any luck, do a little kissing or perhaps go to the local drugstore for a soda and some innocent caressing. It was a vague proposal on Tobe's part, which was met with resistance.

"Tobe," Barbara began, "'stead of comin to my house on Sard'day night, why don't I meet you at the drugstore in the afternoon, say, around three o'clock. I need to talk to you."

"Is sump'n the matter?" Tobe asked, not expecting a departure from the cultural custom. After all, a lot of guys had dates without cars.

"If you wanna see me, it has to be the way I say," she said, showing more character than usual.

"Okay. Fine. Sard'day at three. At the drugstore," Tobe conceded. "I hate that I cain't see you Sard'day night. I mean, I know I ain't got a car and all, but we could still have fun, you know."

"Sard'day at three or not at all," said Barbara as she hung up the phone.

Tobe entered the front door of Holland's Rexall Drugstore on Main Street the following Saturday afternoon after the trial, scanned the room, which was empty except for a couple of soda jerks, saw the top of a blonde head in the far back corner, barely visible, with her back to the room, and aimed himself in her direction after detouring by the soda fountain to pick up a small Coke and tossing the clerk a dime.

Tobe arrived at her booth and tapped her on the top of her head in a feeble attempt at being funny. She turned to look up at him as he announced, "I'm here."

"Hey, Tobe," she responded.

Tobe sat down in the booth seat facing her, smiled, and took a sip of his soda. "What's goin on?" he asked.

"How'd you get here?"

"I hitched a ride."

"Oh. That's nice. Anybody I know?"

"Barbara."

"Yes?"

Tobe saw that she was not very good at acting innocent. *Or is it slow-witted?* he wondered.

"Why could I not go to your house t'night?" Tobe asked.

"Oh, Tobe, I'm so sorry," she whispered.

"What? I'm in the dark."

A long silence ensued as Barbara stared into her soda glass, apparently caught between her genuine infatuation with Tobe and a prohibition to those feelings.

"Barbara?" Tobe inquired gently.

Another pause and then, "Okay, Tobe, here's what happened. I told Daddy all about you, what a nice guy you are, comin from a religious family and all, and how cute you are, and that you even play football for Belhaven High. And he just nodded his head for a while and listened, and then when I was finished and there was this minute of silence, he said, 'So what's Tobe's last name? I wanna know about his family.' So I told him Stanhope was your name. And he got up and walked outta the room."

Silence separated Barbara and Tobe, until Tobe finally found language again.

"Your dad is well-known around town, ain't he?" Tobe knew that her father was a well-established member of the Mount Berry community and was probably aware of everything that went on in this little berg, including well-attended trials.

"His family's been here a long time, yes," she admitted.

"Did he ever come back into the room?"

"Oh yeah. He came back. *Believe me*, he came back."

"So then what?"

"Very simple: he said that I was never to see you agen. Period. End of conversation, and left the room again."

Tobe was silent for a good while—dazed, confused, hurt, startled, and resentful. Finally, he said, "Why?"

"Ain't your uncle the one who is being tried for—" And then it became clear that she did not know what Tobe's uncle was being tried for. "Sump'n—"

"What does that have to do with me?"

"Daddy went to the trial."

"I see," Tobe whispered.

"Tobe, I don't know the details. I just know what my daddy told me what I had to do regardin you. Apparently, he found out thaings about your uncle at the trial he didn't like."

"Well, I guess that's that."

"Tobe, I really do like you—a lot. Unnerstand?"

"Sure," he muttered.

"I gotta go. If somebody sees me here with you, I'm dead." She began sliding across her booth seat. "I'm so sorry, Tobe. Don't be mad at me. I think you're wonderful." And she was gone.

Like two people trying to dance on horses, Tobe thought, and where that thought came from, he had no idea. He played with the straw and the ice cubes in his glass and then remembered the biblical quote, "The son shall not suffer for the iniquity of the father, nor the father suffer for the iniquity of the son. The righteousness of the righteous shall be upon himself, and the wickedness of the wicked shall be upon himself." *Yeah, right.* He remembered the Bible verse memorization competition he had won the year before. "I guess it don't apply to uncles."

A strange feeling began to seep into his body and consciousness, a sense of, what? Loneliness? Of being singled out for no reason; of being prejudiced against without cause; of not being accepted in spite of being his own person; of being found guilty for something he had not done: injustice, outrage. Then, for some strange reason, he began to think about the southern colored folks who were not allowed to go to his school, or eat in his restaurant, or drink out of his water fountain, or go to his church, or, or, or—he felt helpless and was stirred to understanding and compassion for the coloreds. It would leave an indelible, everlasting impression on him of being like those who are not acceptable because of certain whimsical, superficial social criteria.

What a puny concept that alienation of affection is—or any kind of alienation for that matter, which I can now relate to—in a nothin town like this. Anger began to take up residence. And then he thought about the Joads, in whom he always found consolation and perspective. *That's what I'll do. I'll go see The Grapes of Wrath,* and he immediately felt lighter. He plunged into his pocket to count his change and found that he had at least seventy-five cents. *Just enough,* he thought. *The Grapes of Wrath* was becoming his new Bible. He slipped out of the booth, stood tall for a moment, and then marched regally, his head held high, out of the drugstore, the soda jerks staring at him.

Tobe moved on, which is what one does when one is fifteen, or fifty, or five hundred. He did not grieve for Barbara because he knew that she had never been her own person, but suffering discrimination was a new experience. Tobe's father's ancestors, The Stanhopes, had arrived in Virginia on a boat from England in 1625. They were not immigrants; they were merely moving from one part of England to another. His mother's family's burial plot, The Barton's, listed generations of Anglo ancestors. Tobe was the quintessential white Anglo Saxon Protestant boy growing up in a segregated South. His high school graduating class was pure, disgustingly white (*You mean these bunch of poor, redneck, cotton-mill workers' children consider themselves the superior class?* he often thought). Discrimination had never touched him in his sequestered white world of which he was a legitimate member. He would never forget the feeling and would forever after relate to those who endured being singled out for rejection.

After football season was over his sophomore year, having turned fifteen that fall, Tobe's father managed to get him a part-time job with a little corner grocery store in Belhaven, the owner being one of his father's acquaintances. His older brother had also worked for Stroupe's Cash and Carry Groceries (what "cash and carry" designates is that one had the option of paying cash or buying groceries on credit by "carrying" them on the books). It also meant that people could phone in their grocery orders and have their groceries delivered to their home, which also meant that the store had a delivery truck, which Tobe was expected to drive.

The store building was an aged and faded wooden structure with wooden plank floors, which often creaked when walked on, and plate glass windows on the front side. Inside the front door, to the right as one entered, was a long glass counter, Tobe's favorite place, which contained a large assortment of sweets and chocolates (the marketing strategy was to put temptation at the front as one walked in the door), which was abutted by another long counter on which sat the cash register that Tobe learned how to use.

The walls of the store were lined with shelves containing canned food and other dry goods, the middle of the floor had the bread rack and freestanding shelves with more groceries, and in the back of the room was the meat department, which was Mr. Stroupe's pride and joy. He often boasted about having the best cuts of meats in town as well as the best butcher. Tobe spent many hours in this environment, sometimes, depending on Mr. Stroupe's condition, alone managing the whole works with little experience. He felt, because of the lackadaisical management style of Mr. Stroupe, failure for Stroupe's Cash and Carry was inevitable.

"Do you have your driver's license?" Mr. Stroupe asked Tobe during the job interview, which took place in a rather large back room where surplus items were stored and Mr. Stroupe had a desk at which he did his books.

"I have a learner's permit," Tobe told him. He was not sure that Mr. Stroupe was listening, for during the "interview," the owner had opened a desk drawer, taken out a bottle of whiskey, poured himself a glass, returned the bottle, and taken a large gulp.

"That'll do," Mr. Stroupe said after a moment's pause to enjoy the effect of the whiskey.

"But—" Tobe started to say and then realized that he needed this job and that he was quite capable of driving the store's pickup truck, even as ancient as it was and with a stick shift. He estimated the truck to be about twenty years old, and he knew that he would be a little embarrassed in front of his friends, mostly the girls, being seen driving such a dilapidated old truck. But a job was a job, and it would also pay for taking a girl to a movie.

On his first day at work, a Saturday, along about ten thirty, the phone rang at the cash register counter, and Mr. Stroupe took the call. It was an order from one of the wealthiest families in Belhaven, and the owner patiently and politely took precise notes as to what they wanted.

"We'll get that to you right away," Mr. Stroupe said and hung up.

"Shall I get their order together?" Tobe asked.

"You can git started, but we'll wait for more orders. You only need to make one trip a day," the experienced and frugal Mr. Stroupe said.

Mr. Stroupe's store was just across the street from the Chronicle cotton textile mill, and one of Tobe's duties often included waiting on these crushed and defeated textile workers who, when on break or before or after work, were always ordering sodas, chips, wrapped sandwiches,

Johnnie Cakes (basically cookie sandwiches filled with frosting), or Moon Pies, and an assortment of devastatingly unhealthy snack foods and candies from the front counter. (Because of his football training, Tobe had begun to be very health conscious and was appalled by the horrendously bad health habits and the short life expectancy of the citizens in this grindingly poor town.) Many of these workers requested that their bills be placed in the "carry" category, some of whom had accumulated a rather heavy carry load. And so Tobe filled his first day with waiting on the walk-in customers with miniscule transactions while awaiting more phone orders. The phone rang several more times through the middle of the day so that by midafternoon Mr. Stroupe announced that they had enough orders for Tobe to make a run of several deliveries.

Tobe carefully organized the bags of groceries in the bed of the truck, grouping them in four groups according to the house they were to be delivered to, got into the driver's seat in the cab of the truck, checked out the mirror settings, and started the engine. "Piece of cake," he said to himself. Mr. Stroupe had also given him some letters to mail, so his first stop would be the US Post Office.

Since he had only a learner's permit, which allowed him to drive a vehicle only if a licensed driver accompanied him, he was determined that there be no mistakes, that he would drive like an eighty-year-old woman. He eased out of the dirt parking area behind the store, saw no traffic coming from his left, and entered the street turning to the right. He came to the intersection on which the store sat, where he had the green light, and turned right again, headed up Catawba Street toward the intersection at the top of Main Street, where the post office sat at the juncture of the two streets, Main Street running north and south and Catawba Street dead-ending from the east into it, with the post office sitting on Main Street but facing down Catawba Street. He had yet to use his brake pedal.

As he arrived at Main Street, he again had a green light so that he moved slowly under the light and toward the curb directly in front of him. As he approached, he started pressing the brake pedal to stop at the curb. He got no response.

He then began furiously pumping the brake pedal to build up the pressure, but the pressure never came. The brake pedal was all the way to the floor as the front tires hit the curb, jumped over the curb, crossed the sidewalk, and kept moving forward until the truck was on the front lawn of the United States Post Office, where it was stopped by an army recruitment sign, "Uncle Sam Wants You," with Uncle Sam pointing directly in Tobe's face.

"Hey, don't you see that sign that says Keep off the Grass?" a passing stranger said.

Tobe eased it into reverse, looked behind him, where he saw a small group of people had gathered (their first excitement in at least a month), and slowly backed across the sidewalk and into a parking space. He was mortified.

He said to the small group, "I just discovered this truck ain't got no brakes." *With four more stops to make,* he thought. And then of course he received all kinds of advice, from "You better park that thaing and walk" and "You got a bicycle?" to "Next time downshift it into low gear" or "Try to hit reverse." He continued on into the post office to mail the letters and noticed the tire tracks on the lawn and felt guilty for damaging their yard. He also felt lucky to be alive.

Back in the truck and sitting behind the steering wheel in front of the post office, he began to ponder his dilemma, weigh his options, and try to think of a solution. It would never occur to him to return to the store and call it quits, so strong was his sense of duty and responsibility and his respect, or intimidation, for his elders and authority figures.

I've got groceries to deliver, and some thaings in these grocery bags are gonna go bad if I don't deliver them soon, he thought.

He then decided that, one, he would drive very slowly and anticipate stop lights and stop signs well in advance, two, he could double-clutch it into first gear, and, once slow enough, three, he could hit reverse, which should have the effect of stopping its forward progress, and once stopped, he would quickly take it out of reverse.

As he was developing his game plan, his eyes happened to catch sight of the handle of the emergency brakes underneath the dash on the left-hand side next to the door. He reached down and pulled on the brake and felt a little tension, which meant that maybe the emergency brakes could help. With all these thoughts racing through his head, he took a deep breath, muttered, "Here we go," and began slowly backing out of his parking space, committed to his mission.

The rest of the afternoon was a living nightmare and, literally, a death-defying adventure, with only a couple of mishaps. He did end up in one other person's front lawn. In one case he used a tree to stop the truck, in another case he found a street sign to run up against, in another case he found a high curb (curbs being a common device), and the emergency brakes were of some use once he got the truck slowed down to a snail's pace. In retrospect, he knew that he had had a number of close calls and was fortunate just to be alive. This thought needled his consciousness.

Back in the store, Mr. Stroupe was sitting at his desk with a large tumbler of whiskey. His eyes seemed unfocused, as were his hands, which were uncoordinated, knocking objects over and bouncing around purposelessly.

"Mr. Stroupe, I have sump'n to tell you," Tobe began.

"Yeah?" came the slurred response.

"Did you know that your truck ain't got no brakes?"

"Yeah, yeah, I've heard it before," he answered, brushing Tobe off like a pesky fly.

"No, I mean, seriously, absolutely none. I mean, when you hit the brake pedal, it goes all the way to the floor, and nothin happens."

"Did you try pumpin' 'em?" The owner could barely be understood.

"Of course. Nothin' happens," Tobe said with a stronger voice.

"Okay. I'll see what I can do about it t'morra."

"I don't think I can go out in this thaing again."

"T'morra," was Mr. Stroupe's only answer.

Tobe understood that "t'morra" was Sunday, which meant that Mr. Stroupe was merely humoring him and dismissing him. Tobe felt frustration and a touch of anger rising in him like a roiling pot.

There are those moments in life that we know, even at the time that they are happening, are life altering and will never be forgotten. Tobe's experience with the grocery delivery truck was one such experience, which he knew even at the moment. He also knew that he was driving with death sitting next to him in the passenger seat. It may not seem all that dire or dramatic to most people, but Tobe felt that way, that he was living close to death from moment to moment. It is not something a fifteen-year-old can process, having no such previous experience with it and no innate circuitry to deal with it. He also reflected on Mr. Stroupe's irresponsibility and indifference to his dilemma.

Tobe had an agonizing evening and went to bed with jagged thoughts pricking his mind. He felt fortunate to just be alive. He knew also that he would be working for Mr. Stroupe again the next Saturday (during the week, the butcher delivered the groceries—in his own car), and he also sensed that Mr. Stroupe would not remember anything Tobe had told him about the brakes and that the brakes would not be fixed. *What can I possibly do? Who is going to listen to a fifteen-year-old? Where can I find answers?* The thoughts cascaded down through his consciousness and brought up emptiness. He could not find a comfortable position in bed. He fluffed his pillow then shoved it to the floor. He sat up, lay back down, and then sat up again. He needed to go to the bathroom but produced only a trickle. He sat in the rocking chair in his room and rocked and rocked. He wished morning would come, for the night made him feel alone in the universe. Sleep finally captured him in the rocking chair as he succumbed to sheer exhaustion.

Tobe woke up after several hours, and, with a little rest and dawn beginning to decorate the window, he began to take a brighter view. He convinced himself that he survived that first day by his resourcefulness and ingenuity. *I can do it again.* That heartened him. *I thaink I have a strong will to live. Hey, that feels good. Just have faith in m'self. And just maybe I had a little divine providence on my side. That feels really calmin.* Tobe's philosophical and theological spectrum was pretty much limited to the teachings of the Southern Baptist Church in which he had grown up, and he knew little about the universe beyond that. His natural instinct was to turn toward the religion with which he had been indoctrinated, and he discovered why people are so reliant on religion. He felt comforted, but he also had been taught that God has a plan for everybody. He obviously had been spared for a purpose. *What is that purpose? That's what I'll have to find out. What does God want me to do with my life?* And religion lulled him back to sleep.

Tobe was able to make it through the winter and spring working for Mr. Stroupe, driving the wheeled coffin but braced by a stronger seriousness and purposefulness for his life. By late spring, Mr. Stroupe, predictably, declared bankruptcy from "carrying" too much, and Tobe

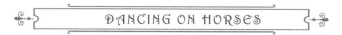

got a position in a local drugstore. During the course of the year, his brother was home on leave from the navy, and when Tobe shared with him the story of the delivery truck, his brother said to him, "You mean he still ain't fixed them brakes?"

CHAPTER 3

"Hey, Dad," Tobe said. His father was standing in Tobe's bedroom in front of a full-length mirror.

"When did I become 'Dad'?" His father turned to him.

"What, you expect me to call you Daddy now? I'm in college, for gosh sake."

"Oh yeah? Well, don't forgit your upbringing. No matter how old you git, you're always beholden to me."

"Yes, Daddy." Tobe grinned.

"What's on your mind?"

Tobe was home for the long Thanksgiving weekend of 1954, the fall of his sophomore year at Mars Hill Junior College located in the stunning mountains of North Carolina, near Asheville. He had chosen this private Baptist junior college because he was not quite ready to give up football yet and felt that he had a chance to get some playing time at a smaller school, which he did his two years there. Moreover, his best buddy, Jack Workman, wanted to attend this same school, so naturally they ended up as roommates. Together they chased women, double-dated, went to class, studied (at least Tobe did), and hung out with other dorm mates. Jack, in fact, had met the love of his life, so he told Tobe. He had quit studying and wanted to get married to Shirley. Tobe tried to warn him about not studying, but Jack was too stricken to think about anything but Shirley.

By Thanksgiving, football season was over, and Tobe knew that his playing days were receding into the past. It was a strange feeling to reflect on how much time, effort, and enthusiasm he had put into playing this game and how important it had been to him, especially as part of his identity in his small town where he and most other football players were sort of hometown heroes. But he was realistic enough to know that he would not be able to play in a four-year college or in the NFL. He had been only average, at best, as a juco player, and his enthusiasm for playing the game evaporated in the mountain air.

The week after his last game, he sat alone on the patio of his dormitory, the mountains blazing with fall ostentatiousness and the air sharp and pure. Tobe ingested the visual feast, and the sheer magnetism of the physical presence mesmerized him into a spiritual awareness, and, surrounded by such wonderment, Tobe had an epiphany. He suddenly became aware that his life was changing its course, and he was suffering a transformation in the present instant; he heard a voice that was so real that it seemed to be totally audible, and he looked around to see if anyone had spoken. He turned inward and listened again in stillness, and out of the silence, the voice said, "I want to become a serious and dedicated student." It was of course the voice from his unconscious, and he knew it, and he sensed in a flash that his life had a new destiny. Without his being aware of it, apparently the educational environment in which he had been swimming had left an impression on him, and this moment had been gestating, unbeknownst to him, in his super-intelligence while he was not listening and was busying his life with other distractions, such as football, which he knew now without a quiver of regret that he was saying goodbye to.

"I been doin' a lotta thinkin' lately."

"Like what?" His father examined his own face closely while talking.

"Like, what am I gonna do with my life—that kinda thing. I mean, I'm finished with football—or it's finished with me—and my life is gonna start goin' in a new direction."

"Okay."

"I've decided I'm gonna become a really good student this fall, make the dean's list and honor society and see where that takes me. I mean, I have been studyin'—some—but not all that hard. Just keepin' my head above water—grade-wise," Tobe explained.

"You mean I been wastin' my money?" His dad was satisfied with himself in the mirror by now.

"No. I been layin' a foundation, but I'm ready now to really git my head into being a super student."

Silence ensued while Tobe processed the conversation thus far. He was trying to decide how far he wanted to go with this confessional, just how much of his soul he wanted to bare. Tobe wanted to tell his father about his epiphany. The father was cleaning his fingernails.

"I wanna ask you something."

"Okay." His father did not look up from his preoccupation.

Tobe took a deep breath. "How do you know when God is talkin' to you?"

Another long silence followed, and then Tobe's dad said, "I gotta take a shit."

Tobe waited in his father's bedroom and opened his English literature textbook which he had brought home with him. He was enrolled in a British-literature survey course that semester covering from the Romantics to the moderns and was currently studying Keats. He read:

> Then felt I like some watcher of the skies
> When a new planet swims into his ken:
> Or like stout Cortez when with eagle eyes
> He stared at the Pacific—and all his men
> Looked at each other with a wild surmise—
> Silent upon a peak in Darien.

He closed the book in reverence as his father reentered the room.

"Now, where were we?"

"You needed to take a shit." Tobe flicked him a smile.

"Before that. You said sump'n about how do you know when God is talkin' to you."

"Right."

"Do you think God has spoke to you?"

"That's what I'm askin' you. I think so, but—how do I know for sure?"

"Well, I would say that it's just a real powerful feelin' about sump'n. It just kinna presses on your mind, and you become convinced that it's the right thaing for you," his father explained. "Has that happened to you?"

"I was just tellin' you about bein' finished with football and takin' a whole new direction in my life and becomin' a good student," Tobe repeated.

"To what end?"

"Sir?"

"So you become a good student and make good grades—and then what? For what purpose?"

Tobe had not seen that far ahead. For him, at this point, learning was an exciting end in itself, and he relished the intellectual stimulation and the challenge—like the competition and challenge of football, a goal of its own. An education, he had heard professors say, is an end in itself, because it makes you a better person, and he believed it. They sat in silence for a little while again while they each mulled over the subject.

And then his father spoke.

"Have you ever thought about becomin a minister?"

"A min—" Tobe stopped.

"A preacher. A Southern Baptist preacher."

"I guess—it's crossed my mind—but—"

"I jest want you to know that nuthin would make me happier and more proud of you. Don't you forget it. *Nuthin* would make me more proud."

Tobe's incubator, nursery, nurturer, natural environment, and teacher had been the Southern Baptist Church, so the thought was not a stranger to him. He had sat through untold numbers of sermons, done thousands of Sunday school lessons, memorized endless passages of biblical scripture, absorbed all the stories from the Bible, including God's plan for humankind and salvation, had done daily devotions all his life, and was totally immersed, or brainwashed, in the ways of theology, ecclesiasticism, and religion.

"We're both gonna git down on our knees and go to the throne of God to ask for His guidance. I'm gonna pray for you, and I want you to pray also. We'll find out what God wants you to do with your life," his dad said, concluding the conversation.

Tobe returned to college after the Thanksgiving holiday with a new dedication to his studies and a confused state about his life's compass. During his course of study at college, as far as the coeds were concerned, he had dated around casually but never felt any real dynamics with any girl in particular. He was a free-ranging rooster and open to suggestion, which came in the form of his college pal Earl. Earl, a freshman in college, in Tobe's eyes was a good guy, friendly, witty, easy to hang out with, and one heck of an athlete, running track and a champion in the hundred-yard dash, clocking a 10.4.

"Hey, Tobe, I'm goin' home next weekend to see my girlfriend. You wanna come with me?" Earl, who lived in the same dorm as Tobe, asked as they were walking back to the dorm one early winter day after class.

"Didn't you just see her at Thanksgiving?" Tobe teased, aware that his language was changing.

"Yeah, but I can't live without her very long."

"Well, I probably should stay here and study. We're gettin close to finals,"

Tobe responded, familiar with the pattern that the semester did not end until after Christmas, final exams torturing in January.

"You got the whole Christmas holidays to study, buddy. Besides, she's got a girl friend who wants to meet you. We showed her your picture. Trust me, man; this gal is drop-dead gorgeous. She won the Miss Teen South Carolina beauty contest. You'll thank me for the rest of your life."

"Oh yeah?" Tobe was not so easily lured away from his newfound dedication to erudition.

Tobe was skeptical about Earl's description and enthusiasm but, realizing that he still had a month to study before finals, decided to toss a weekend into the garbage, have a little change of scenery away from campus (and campus food), and go with Earl back to Earl's hometown, Spartanburg, South Carolina, which served as the footstool of the Blue Ridge Mountains, which sloped down from North Carolina. For Tobe, the excursion down the mountain compensated for any time spent away from the library studying; it was early December, the mountain atmosphere was choked with beauty and tranquility, and the road from Asheville to Spartanburg, one that Tobe had never taken, gashed through hills of stunning wonderment.

It was late Saturday morning, after their Saturday classes, the usual configuration of classes being Tuesday, Thursday, Saturday, the alternative to Monday, Wednesday, Friday, which created a challenge for Tobe and the rest of the football team in the fall when there was a game on Saturday afternoons. By Saturday noon, for everybody, the grind of the week was discarded and freedom embraced. The ride down the North

Carolina mountains, which Tobe had been devoted to since childhood, was a sort of sacred journey for him, forgetting about chemistry and US government classes and just breathing deeply. Besides, Earl was easy to be with and had a vast repertoire of jokes and humor—and had, as far as Tobe could tell, exquisite taste in women (having met Earl's girlfriend).

Tobe and Earl had a mere twenty-four hours to spend in Spartanburg, having to commence their return journey to campus by Sunday, midafternoon, for the two-hour drive back into Tobe's wondrous mountains. At home, Earl's number-one priority was not his parents but his girlfriend, Cheryl, whose number-one asset, although she was quite attractive, was her breasts. Tobe recalled that in one late-night bull session, Earl muttered something about how much he loved breasts, that he could "marry a pair of tits" for no other reason (the guys were all in that glandular stage). Tobe's impression was that Cheryl, rather fleshy, would someday be an overweight woman, but Earl was totally enamored and oblivious.

At Earl's house, Earl made some phone calls, and soon thereafter, the two of them were in the car on their way to Cheryl's house where Bettyjean would be present.

Spartanburg, which got its name from the Spartan Regiment of the Revolutionary War and the nearby Battle of Cowpens, stood as a gleaming little town of idyllic patina, quiet suburbs of well-attended lawns, a small, classic liberal arts college, a quaint and antique downtown area composed of local ownership instead of giant chains, an historic county courthouse and square, and the ubiquitous shanty town on the other side of the tracks, that colored universe that in 1954 was largely hidden in all southern towns. Like many towns of that region, it contained a lot of history, especially of the Revolutionary War that was fought throughout the area, and it was also a cotton textile town because of the abundance of water power and cheap labor (and no unions); it was nicknamed the "Lowell of the South" and also "The Hub" because of the railroads.

Tobe and Earl passed through neighborhoods of Victorian vintage and aimed at Cheryl's home, a historical and well-preserved bungalow. Cheryl greeted them at the door with a hug for Earl, an embarrassingly lengthy and intimate embrace. While this was happening, Tobe was inclined to look away and actually glanced over their shoulders further into the room where he saw a teenage goddess standing. *Holy shit!* Tobe thought. *Earl was not lying.*

Earl and Cheryl finally let go of their embrace, and Cheryl said, "Tobe, I want you to meet Bettyjean. Bettyjean"—she faced her friend—"this is Tobe, Earl's college buddy." Tobe's heart was dancing, but his body stiffened into rigor mortis.

"Okay, buddy," Earl prompted after a silent moment, "you're supposed to say something like, 'Nice to meet you,' or something. You know the dance."

Tobe never felt so socially inadequate in his life because his mind was gyroscoping while his mouth was locked.

Bettyjean came forward and offered Tobe a handshake. Tobe mustered up enough presence to accept it while staring at her face and thinking, *She is the most gorgeous creature I have ever seen. My God. I think I'm in love already. I want to hold her and hold on to her—forever.*

He surmised she was about seventeen years old. Tobe first looked at her eyes, which were so blue they looked unreal. He scanned her skin, which was satiny looking, and then he observed that she had a dainty nose, a heart-shaped face, dark brown hair, and a smile, which when she engaged it, moved Tobe's heart to near tears it was so sweet and innocent. Tobe, being five feet eleven, had to look down a few inches to her face and guessed that she was of average female height, *a perfect fit,* he thought, with a body that stopped just short of voluptuousness. *I can't believe my luck.*

"Nice to meet you, Tobe," Bettyjean said, still holding his hand.

"Come on, ole Tobe, you can do it," Earl teased him.

"Nice to meet you, J—J—Janecrumbs." Tobe was able to unlock his jaw enough to embarrass himself, and everyone released a horselaugh.

"Bettyjean," she corrected. Tobe felt the blood in his face and the heat in his cheeks.

"I'm sorry," he said. "I was so taken with your face that I wasn't payin'—I'm so stupid—I'm sorry, if you'll forgive me." He calculated that humility and honesty might be a better wager.

"It's okay. I understand."

What a great start, Tobe thought, determined to somehow atone for his blunder.

"Tell you what: why don't you two sit on the porch swing, and me and Cheryl will run down to the Spigot Ice Cream place and bring us some ice cream," Earl said. It was never too cool for ice cream.

While Tobe and Bettyjean moved from the living room to the front porch swing, Tobe drew on his old football experience of right before kickoff or in the huddle when his play had been called and took several very deep, relaxing breaths and tried to visualize outcomes, which he had become pretty good at—but apparently not good enough for the NFL. At least he wore his college letter sweater as well as his football conditioning. He visualized himself sitting next to Bettyjean, relaxed, confident, witty, intelligent, sexy, the college man with a lowly high school student, being her superior. They sat down and swung lightly in the southern early-winter, chilly air, the Garden of Eden, the first couple, the ancient dance.

"So, Bettyjean," he began confidently, "what grade are you in?"

"I'm a junior," she said softly. Tobe was so thrilled by her voice that he didn't catch the question she asked next. He allowed a silent moment to intervene and then tried to pick up the remnants of their conversation.

"I'm just working on basics right now. No major yet."

"But, I mean, what are you preparing yourself for?"

"Life," the sophisticated college man replied.

"But what do you want to be?"

"An intelligent, fulfilled human being."

A lot of quiet spaces noisily protruded in their dialogue.

"Oh." And silence ensued again. Tobe wondered if he had been too glib while she seemed, to Tobe, to dance round the edges of confusion, uncertain what to make of him.

"You know what I want to be?" she said.

Tobe judged that she was not a coy, coquettish, devious, game-playing teenage airhead. She seemed a solid young lady in terms of her convictions about life. "I'd be interested to know." Tobe noted that she seemed to be self-assured—and liked it.

"I want to be a preacher's wife," she stated simply and sincerely.

Rigor mortis set in again, and the universe stood still. Tobe struggled. Tingles and shivers filled his body. It was the rapture, an epiphany, a Garden of Gethsemane, Golgotha, the ascension—all in one. After a few moments, he found words.

"I'm a ministerial student," Tobe whispered, thinking, *At least I am now*, lying but not lying. And his life took a new path. He decided then and there that he was going to announce himself for the ministry and declare himself on his senior college application forms as a pre-ministerial student, and thought, *I'm going to apply myself to my studies like I have never done before—like football practice in August*. He felt like doing something noble, brave, brilliant, like a cure for cancer (or writing a moving sermon), for the sake of a beautiful lady just to sway her. He thought about the medieval literature he had studied and the motivation engendered in knights by beautiful ladies, and just as silly, he thought. He had done many things in his short lifetime to impress a girl—on the diving board, on the football field, in a drag race, in the weight room, around the campus, at a dance—but this was a first, to become a preacher as a way of capturing a girl's heart. And he felt no shame, even though an unnamed worm squirmed somewhere in the depths of his unconscious. He also felt just a twinge of silliness, his intelligence making a judgment call.

As part of all this decision making that was happening in the present moment, Tobe determined that he would become a philosophy major in order to prepare himself for theological studies, even though he had already considered philosophy as a possible major. He also felt a degree of dishonesty because he was making a gigantic decision under the influence of this incredibly pulchritudinous, angelic face.

"Seriously?" she quietly asked with slight astonishment in her voice, turning to look at Tobe to see whether he was jesting with her.

"Seriously," Tobe said with all the sincerity he could muster. "I've been thinkin' about it for a long time and just recently reached a decision." He knew that he was not lying about that since he had just this moment made the decision.

"You know you're very handsome, don't you, Tobe?"

Tobe reddened with pleasure. *Encouraging,* thought Tobe. "I think we might have something special goin' on here." *How can I not do everything in my power to get this girl? Any guy would.*

Earl and Cheryl walked up the steps and onto the porch, Earl clutching a container of Spigot Ice Cream. "Let's eat," he said.

Inside, they sat around the dining room table over bowls of ice cream and clinking spoons, Tobe and Bettyjean slyly and shyly stealing looks at each other but hiding nothing from the other couple. The glow on both their faces was too luminescent to suppress, and Tobe thought, *Is this what it feels like to be in love? I'll bet it is,* still trying to talk himself into it, based solely on her beauty.

"Cheryl," Tobe began, "can we go to the Morgan Street Baptist Church in the morning?" Bettyjean had mentioned in one of Tobe's silent moments that she played the piano for their church.

"Are you outta your mind?" Earl exploded.

"We *are* goin'," Cheryl responded and then looked at Earl. "*All* of us."

"Thanks a lot, Tobe," Earl said.

"And Sunday school too. Y'all are gonna pick us up at nine thirty"— Cheryl turned to Earl—"on time."

"What the"—Earl paused—"what is your interest in the Morgan Street Baptist Church?"

"Bettyjean is the church pianist there. I wanna hear her play," Tobe explained.

"Do you realize we have to git back to campus before dark?"

"We'll make it with your drivin'," Tobe said.

"Why don't you and Bettyjean walk out on the porch," Earl suggested after the ice cream bowls and spoons were put away. "Me and Cheryl wanna say good night in a proper fashion."

On the porch, Tobe said to Bettyjean, "We may be out here awhile."

"I don't think so," Bettyjean said. "I know Cheryl. She's a good girl."

"But Earl's not a good boy." Tobe laughed.

Silence then hung in the air of a southern December late afternoon, just at sunset, with radiance falling down all around them.

"Would it be askin' too much if I ask you for a hug?" Tobe ventured.

"Of course not," Bettyjean answered, with her arms lifted and outward. And so they hugged, sweetly, innocently, reverently for a few silent minutes.

"I just want you to know," Tobe said, "something really important happened to me today."

"Me too," Bettyjean said. And then they savored the look and the touch of each other.

"We're out of here," Earl said as he emerged through the door.

In the car, Earl tried hard to make conversation, but Tobe was not inclined. He was in a different universe and not even a parallel one.

"What's the matter? Cat got your tongue?"

No response.

"Aw, come on, Tobe. I take it you guys hit it off?"

Tobe smugly embraced his secret and his silence.

"Hey, Tobe, what's with this church business?" Earl asked.

Tobe was still struggling to formulate a sentence that would best describe what had happened to him.

"I told Bettyjean that I'm studying for the ministry."

"You fucker! You'll do anything for a piece of ass, won't you?" Earl laughed.

"It's never free." Tobe laughed, contentedly sharing the idiocy of the male ego, especially one who had just turned nineteen. Using church to chase girls was not foreign to Tobe, being an instinctual reaction, an extension of a lifetime behavior pattern. *Church and girls always go together,* Tobe thought, *church always being a great place to pick up women with their guard down, always assuming they can trust you as a Christian boy.*

Tobe began to hum, and then he whistled for a little while, attempting somehow to express what was happening to him. And then he began to sing the Four Aces' "Love Is a Many Splendored Thing" and then switched to the McGuire Sisters' "Sincerely." "Oh, you know how much I love you," he sang, and then he let out a very un-Baptist cry of venality. "Ohhhhh shiiiit!"

"Ain't you embarrassed?" Earl said.

"Ain't *you*, considering your conduct?" Tobe said.

Then they joined in a smug, pal-sharing, cleansing laugh.

Cheryl and Bettyjean's Sunday school class was in the basement of the Morgan Street Baptist Church—a church, so thought Tobe, that greatly resembled East Belhaven Baptist Church. But then again, many Southern Baptist churches had similar architectural features: redbrick exterior walls, white columns on a wide and high front porch, stained glass windows, and the ubiquitous steeple at the front of a pitched roof. The classroom that they were in was fairly small with a ring of folding chairs around three walls, a blackboard and a small lectern beside the only door. The room had no windows, while the walls consisted of painted plaster in a dull, pale, nondescript color. Tobe, sitting next to one of the walls, thought that he could feel a severe coldness emanating from it, and he noticed that, being belowground, moisture trickled down the wall in places like cold tears. Sometimes churches depressed Tobe as he tried to ignore his reaction. Tobe was vaguely aware that deep in his unconscious he basically recoiled from such a joyless and oppressive institution that he was constantly forced into.

Earl introduced Tobe to the rest of the members of Cheryl and Bettyjean's Sunday school class. "This is my friend from college, Tobe Stanhope. He is a pre-ministerial student and football player for Mars Hill." Tobe was certain that he detected a tone of sarcasm in Earl's voice about the "pre-ministerial student" nomenclature but under the circumstances could not reprimand him the way he would like to. Earl continued to see how far he could push his buddy. "And if I have anything to do with it, he'll be elected most handsome for the yearbook this year."

"Don't do that, Earl," Tobe said, editorializing quietly.

Bettyjean spoke up from the other side of the circle they were sitting in. "And I bet he wins it too." Tobe looked at her to see whether she was joining Earl's sarcasm game, but she was totally straight-faced. Tobe was lifted.

The Sunday school teacher, standing behind the lectern, stepped in and looked at Tobe. "Since you are a ministerial student, why don't you lead us in a word of prayer before we start with today's lesson."

Tobe's first thought was, *Oh shit,* and then his mind turned to scrambled eggs while he swore he would get even with Earl. But it was kickoff time, so he took a deep breath, visualized success, and proceeded on his well-trained Southern Baptist instincts. "Let us pray," he began in a sonorous Southern Baptist voice. "Our heavenly Father, we thank You for this beautiful Sabbath morning and for the wonderful Christian fellowship that we have been enjoying and the freedom we have to worship You. We thank You for all the many blessings that You have bestowed upon us, and we are humbled by Your generosity and forgiveness. We pray for those who are less fortunate than we are and for all those lost souls who have not found their way to Thee. We pray that You will help us lead them to Jesus so that they too may be saved. In Jesus's name we pray. Amen." Amen, amen multiplied and scurried around the room. Tobe knew the doctrine well and felt fraudulent. He had also learned that when one prays, one does all the talking without ever really listening to God, *a curious thing*, he often thought.

"That was so beautiful," Bettyjean whispered, and guilt flooded Tobe.

"I've had enough of church for today," Earl whispered to Tobe after the class was over. "Let's go."

"The whole purpose in coming here was to hear Bettyjean play the piano in the worship service," Tobe argued. "We can't leave now."

"I—" Earl stopped his reply upon the arrival of Bettyjean and Cheryl.

"What is everyone doing after the preaching service today?" Bettyjean asked the two young college men.

"We gotta git back to school," said Earl, eager to get started.

"My mother has a fabulous dinner cooked," Bettyjean said. "You have to eat first."

"We'll git something on the road," Earl said.

Tobe diplomatically offered clarification. "We don't wanna put you to any trouble."

"My mother does this every Sunday," Bettyjean said. "It's already cooked. Now come on. My sister and her husband will be there too."

"We'd be delighted to accept your invitation," Tobe said, trying to be gracious.

"*Tobe*"—Earl lightly punched Tobe on the shoulder—"we gotta git goin'."

"Cheryl, we need your help." Tobe turned to Earl's girlfriend.

"Come on, Earl. I wanna be with you a little longer." Cheryl touched Earl's arm, and the battle was over.

"Oh, okay," Earl conceded.

"We'll meet you after church, and you can follow us to my house. I've got to go play the piano for church," Bettyjean explained as she turned and walked away, Tobe eyeing her well-formed and ample bottom in departure. He thought, *Yummmh*.

"Thanks, Earl," Cheryl said to him. "I've got to go sing in the choir this morning." And then she departed.

"I think Bettyjean's hot for you," Earl whispered to Tobe.

"The feelin's mutual."

"You two would make a gorgeous couple."

"She'd certainly hold up her end of the deal," Tobe said.

The Godwin dining room was the embodiment of elegance with a lace tablecloth spread over a mahogany dining table with eight armed chairs around it and a brilliant crystal chandelier hanging above the table with silver, crystal, and fine china place settings perfectly and orderly arranged around the edges of the table. A massive breakfront containing the family heirlooms stood sentry against one wall. Mrs. Godwin made the proper appointments, putting Tobe and Bettyjean together on one side, Earl and Cheryl together on the other side, and Bettyjean's sister and brother-in-law, who looked and sounded like Bing Crosby, across from each other, with Mrs. Godwin standing at the head of the table. Mr. Godwin's chair, at the opposite end of the table from Mrs. Godwin, was empty.

"Let's all join hands," said Mrs. Godwin as they encircled the table.

"Let's let Tobe say the blessing," suggested Bettyjean. "He prays so beautifully."

Tobe defined Southern Baptist social events as, *when all else fells, say a prayer,* and suppressed the thought.

Kickoff time again, thought Tobe. He swallowed hard, cleared his throat, took a deep breath, visualized, and hauled himself onto the field. "Let us bow our heads.

"Our heavenly Father," Tobe began. (*He must be getting tired of hearing from me by now*) "We thank Thee for the wonderful hospitality offered by this fine Christian home, and we pray Your blessings on every member of this wonderful family. Now bless this food to the nourishment of our bodies and our bodies to Thy service. In Jesus's name we pray. Amen." Amen, amen, amen intoned the others.

"Praise Jesus," said Mrs. Godwin.

This is getting out of hand, Tobe thought, *but if I'm going to be a preacher, I need to get used to it*—and something subtly stiffened and resisted inside of him.

Just as Mrs. Godwin was starting to pass the mashed potatoes around the table, a bang came from the front of the house, like maybe a door being slammed angrily, announcing someone's arrival. "Oh no," whispered Bettyjean.

Mrs. Godwin calmly rose from her chair and moved gracefully and patiently through the swinging door into the living room. Silence spread across the dining room table, and Tobe wondered about the loud voices that crept through the door, both male and female.

"Pass the potatoes please," Bing Crosby said, and his wife added, "Yes, let's proceed as though there is not a worry in the world," and everyone began to pass and serve.

The voices had muted on the other side of the door, and then cautiously the door pushed open, and Mr. and Mrs. Godwin entered slowly, he unsteadily, supported by his wife.

"Everyone, this is Mr. Godwin. It appears we spent a little too much time at the nineteenth hole at the country club," she explained, making no effort to conceal his condition.

"Damn right. I shot a seventy-six for the first time, and I celebrated it," Mr. Godwin slurred. "I'm ready for the PGA tour." Everyone looked at their food and tried to eat.

"Now, Bill, just sit at the other end of the table and get some food in you. You'll be all right in a few minutes. And try not to talk," Mrs. Godwin said gently.

She appeared to know what worked best, and Tobe surmised that it was not confrontation. Tobe also observed that Bill Godwin, in spite of his condition, was respectful of his wife. Tobe noted that Godwin was a rather bulky man as compared to his wife, who was quite diminutive, but she was in total control, forceful, decisive, smart, and, above all, Christlike, the very heart and soul of goodness, Tobe judged, which was probably what intimidated Mr. Godwin the most. Tobe could tell that he was trying his best to cover his condition, talking about his golf game, the weather, but mostly about Caterpillar equipment and their wonders, he owning a Caterpillar dealership. It was clear that he had a passion for heavy equipment.

"We need to be getting on the road," Earl said after dessert. "We've got a long drive ahead of us." And then it was all about goodbyes.

Bettyjean walked Tobe to the car and apologized for her father.

"Hey," said Tobe, "he's not your responsibility. Don't give it a second thought."

"You probably don't ever want to see me again after that demonstration."

"Are you nuts? I wish I could take you with me right now," Tobe said.

And thus began a wildly passionate, ecstatic, euphoric, rapturous, joyful, blissful albeit long-distance romance between Tobe and Bettyjean. Tobe was convinced that he had found the love of his life and thought she had too. He affirmed his commitment by announcing to the congregation of East Belhaven Baptist Church, when he came home for the Christmas holidays, that he had been called by God to be a preacher and was henceforth to be considered, officially, a pre-ministerial student in college, studying for the Baptist ministry.

Over the next two years, on a parallel track, something else was happening to Tobe, something going completely against the grain of his announcement to Bettyjean, his parents, who were ecstatic about his career choice, and the Baptist community. The creature that squirmed deep inside his soul was the awareness that he was too venal to make this stick, too fond of female flesh and good times. He suddenly thought of Jacob in Genesis who, when he was alone, began to wrestle with a messenger from God till daybreak, and when the messenger saw that he could not overpower Jacob, he touched Jacob's hip and wrenched it. Tobe touched his hip, to check it out, and began his wrestling match with God.

In his newly discovered territory of college erudition, Tobe was doubly motivated to devote his energies to his studies and with a high degree of excitement and dedication.

After the Christmas holidays, Tobe returned to school to finish the fall semester's final exams in January and prepared for them like he had never done before; by the time exams were over, on a Friday afternoon, he was confident that he had done well, knowing the answers to every question on every final. Final grades were handed out within a week, and Tobe scored a perfect 4.0 for the fall semester.

I knew I had it in me, he thought upon receipt of the notice that he had made the dean's list and the honor society and began to discover a whole new world of books, libraries, ideas, knowledge, and learning, more thrilling in their seduction than football and girls. It was, in fact, a rebirth for him but not of the Christian-born-again kind. A new maturity and confidence began to emerge for Tobe, one of those pivots in life one occasionally encounters.

His friend Jack's life spiraled in the opposite direction. Neglecting his studies and mesmerized by Shirley, Jack was asked not to return to the college. He slinked back to their hometown, was hired by Tobe's father, who was now in the life insurance business as a district manager, married the woman he adored, and had no desire to finish college. But Tobe knew that they would remain friends forever, regardless of their divergent paths.

When Tobe in the fall enrolled in Wake Forest University, one of the finest private schools in the South, albeit Baptist, he declared, as he had already decided, his major as philosophy, the systematic study of the search for truth and love of learning. To this point in time, his philosophical training was based in the Southern Baptist Church and the Holy Bible: he had been taught that the world is six thousand years old, that God in the likeness of a man stepped out and said, "Hocus pocus," and there was, and that God is very involved in Tobe's daily life, as in "Help me make this touchdown," "Help me pass this test," "Help me cure my cold," (as though God did not have more important business) watching down through a peep hole in the sky and directing his life like a puppet on a string (the Baptist propaganda was that God is always watching us).

Tobe was introduced for the first time in his young life to the history of Western humankind's search for ultimate truth and reality; to such questions as, what is reality; to thought systems that did not rely on God for answers and which in fact left God pretty much out of the picture; to the inquiries of Socrates (who wondered if a gnat buzzed through its nose or its anus, according to Aristophanes), Plato, and Aristotle; to epicureanism, stoicism, and skepticism; to rationalism, realism, and pantheism; to empiricism, epistemology, and materialism; to pragmatism, positivism, and phenomenology; to metaphysics, scientific and inductive thinking, and existentialism—an unending flood tide of thought and theory, with no truth anywhere visible. He became immersed in his studies and asking questions that he had never even known existed. Tobe's universe exploded exponentially, and he began asking questions with no answers, far beyond anything he had ever thought before. He was confronted with scientific, geological, anthropological, biological, archeological, astrological, philosophical (Nietzsche's statement that "God is dead" undermined everything he had been taught), theological truths. In his Latin class, he discovered the classical ideal of *mens sana in corpore sano*, "a healthy mind in a healthy body." It was something he could hold on to with some sense of sanity. He was shaken to his foundations and broadened.

But it was not a philosopher who changed Tobe's entire outlook on life and the universe. It was in an anthropology class that he was assigned to read Darwin's *The Origin of the Species*. He began it late one afternoon in the library, and once started, could not stop. The anthropology class had already rattled his faith, and Darwin merely added to his torment. He was slowly learning that the earth was in fact almost five billion years old (so long to God saying, "Abracadabra"), that life began with a lightning bolt (adios to God making the first human from clay), and that the human species evolved from lower life forms (goodbye, Adam and Eve). Tobe stayed with Darwin on through the dinner hour and well into the night, almost finishing the five hundred pages by one o'clock in the morning. He was traumatized and did not sleep the rest of the night. God had been totally left out of the picture, and he felt abandoned, alone, vulnerable, and depressed.

Education is a destructive process, as Tobe was learning, but he was determined to keep exploring and learning. But the deeper he moved into intellectual enlightenment, the further he moved away from the God of the Southern Baptist Church and deeper into a spiritual crisis.

"You," Tobe answered simply one day in a discussion with his favorite philosophy professor. Tobe had been revealing to the young professor his doubts about the whole question of God and Christianity; the professor was shocked, wanting to know, "What led you to doubt your faith?"

Professor Brown was stunned by Tobe's revelation. "Me?" he asked. "What did I do?"

"You presented the whole realm of philosophical thought in such an objective and rational manner that I was able to make my own decision, based on what I had learned about philosophy."

It was a magical and scary interval in his life, fired by new ideas, new ways of thinking, and daily new encounters. His father thought that the school had corrupted him—and so it had, in the same way that Socrates had corrupted the youth of Athens, according to the charges against him and for which he was served hemlock.

Tobe was a young man without a place in the universe. On the one hand, he had stood before the congregation and publically declared that God had whispered in his ear to be a preacher (just as he had been maneuvered into proclaiming that he had been saved when he was twelve years old); on the other hand, he knew that he had made a mistake and that he could never, ever be a minister, unless he became the greatest hypocrite that ever trod on the planet. He prayed, he meditated, he read the Bible, he talked to other ministerial students, he talked to ministers, he talked to faculty members, he talked to career counselors, and he prayed some more, and then prayed some more.

"Our nada who art in nada, nada be thy nada." He thought of the waiter's prayer in Hemingway's "A Clean, Well-Lighted Place." He thrashed about in his sleep at night, he took long runs for clarity sake, he had nightmares, he read great literature—Shakespeare, Chaucer, the Romantic poets, especially Blake the mystic—to find peace and inspiration, and he drifted further away from his original commitment and his religious instructions and closer to a decision.

After all his search for truth, what he came to recognize is that nobody knows the truth, no matter what preachers, monks, bishops, or the popes say. They are just human beings with a lot of faith. He reached the conclusion that the study of philosophy is like being in a coal mine at midnight on a moonless night, searching for a black cat that isn't there. Blackness overtook him in his little white world.

"Have faith," he was told ad nauseam. "Faith in what?" he repeated ad nauseam. "I need a starting point," he pled. "Cogito ergo sum," advised Descartes. "That's not my problem," he said aloud to himself. "I know that I exist. I breathe, I eat, I smell, I feel—I shit, therefore I am." *My existence does not prove anything, except that I exist,* he thought. Blackness.

I cannot stand up on a Sunday morning in a Southern Baptist church and say, "Uncertainty is the basic fact of human existence. Please come forward and be saved." That won't jerk any souls to Jesus. I can't promise that we are all going to a paradisial existence called heaven after we die and live happily, eternally after—if we are all good little boys and girls. I can't make that promise. In fact, I can't promise anything—those thoughts being the only thing that Tobe was certain of.

If he were the minister of a church, he pondered, what could he promise them? Blackness, uncertainty, doubt, and nothing to believe in? Goodbye to ministry, goodbye to the Baptist Church, goodbye to the Judeo-Christian God, goodbye to dualism, and, yes, goodbye to philosophy; hello, universe.

Holy shit. What the fuck am I gonna do now? was all he could think, in not exactly the language of a Baptist preacher.

The bad news about his relationship with Bettyjean was that they got to see each other on rare occasions, special weekends, holidays, vacations, summers, and whatever else they could manage (but when they were together, it was passionate, physical, with heavy petting and dangerous moves). The good news was that he had no distractions from his studies. One long weekend that fall semester, he went to visit Bettyjean, who was in her senior year in high school and making plans to apply to Wake Forest to be close to Tobe. Tobe felt the walls closing in from all directions, but he was not ready to share with her what had happened in his life, for he knew the moment he announced he was no longer a ministerial student would be the moment she would walk away. *Should I continue to be a ministerial student in order to hold on to such beauty?* Dishonesty was not his style, and his heart sank at the recognition.

CHAPTER 4

"Dad." Tobe approached his father, who was standing in the family den where Tobe had spent many childhood hours reading in the big red lounge chair. Tobe was home for Christmas break in his junior year, and the family was getting ready to go out to dinner at a local fish camp. His father was looking in the smallish mirror in the den room hung in the midst of some family portraits.

"Yes, son," he answered as he continued perfecting his tie knot.

"I need to talk to you."

"Go ahead."

"Maybe this isn't the right time," Tobe said, backing off from a difficult subject.

"We got a few minutes," his father encouraged him.

"Well, Dad, I don't know. I'm havin' a really hard time right now."

"With your studies?"

"No, no. My studies are fine. In fact, they are doin' great. I've got close to a 4.0 goin' into finals. But …"

"But?"

"I think I might have misunderstood what God has been sayin' to me."

"About what?"

Tobe decided to see if he could lighten the moment.

"Well, I thought God said preacher, but what he actually said was teacher. I got it straight now. He wants me to teach preachers. It was a very confusing message, you know, teach/preach, but I now understand what God wants me to do with my life." Tobe inhaled deeply, unjangled his nervous system, and then leaned into the smooth feeling; he immediately felt as though he was lighter by at least a ton and could just float right off the ground. He was also proud of his honesty.

"You know what I thaink? I thaink that *liberal* school has ruined you. They've corrupted your mind. They've put all kinds of atheistic ideas in your head. That's what I tha

ink," his father said. Tobe had been debating theology with his father since being home for Christmas—a bad mistake.

"No, Dad. The school hasn't done anything—"

"They've ruined you—that's what they've did, after I've spent my life teachin' you right from wrong and all about God."

"Dad, I'm my own person now—"

"Let's go eat." He turned and walked out the door.

"My truth is my truth," Tobe mumbled and followed his father—reluctantly. He was still looking forward to some fried catfish. Philosophy had not stolen all his southern culture.

As Tobe moved away from theological thought and philosophical inquiry, he moved imperceptibly toward literary studies, which had always been a secret passion since early childhood with his mystical summer afternoons of reading and book adventures. Tobe remembered taking a class in the Romantic poets, especially Keats (while Byron remained his scandalous hero) when he was a senior in high school, which elevated his passion for reading to a new level and left an indelible imprint on his soul. Tobe kept this side of himself to himself for fear of being scoffed at, but in honest moments, he admitted his duality and tried to maintain the façade of a normal teenage boy, which he was fairly successful at. He had been popular enough to be elected senior class president, he was good enough as a football player to be in the starting lineup (on offense), and he had participated in normal teen activities such as cruising, hanging out, hot-rodding, and dating (especially dating). Tobe was aware from an early age, unlike his high school classmates, that Belhaven was a culturally deprived, anemic, dull, bleak little town with limited opportunities and promise. Great literature had shown him other possibilities.

"Tobe," came the voice on the other end of the phone line, "this is Jack."

Tobe was still home for Christmas break and had already been to visit

Jack and Shirley, who were now living in a small apartment in the county seat where Tobe's dad's insurance office was.

"Yeah, Jack, what's going on?"

"Last Sunday, me and Shirley went to have lunch with my aunt, you know, my dad's sister, over in White Mountain. So she invited us to go to church with her before goin out to lunch," Jack explained.

"Okay."

"She goes to the First Baptist Church of White Mountain where Dr. Sternbridge, a friend of my dad's, is the minister," Jack continued.

"Uh-huh."

"Well, after church, I was talkin' to the minister's daughter, Anne Sternbridge, who I know slightly, and she asked me in the course of the conversation if I knew anybody that was goin' toward Raleigh after Christmas break. She goes to that girls' school there—you know, Meredith College."

"It's called the Angel Farm, being right next to a cow pasture that belongs to NC State," Tobe said.

"She said she needs a ride back to school and wanted to know if I knew anybody that happened to be goin' in that direction, and I immediately thought of you. How are you gittin back?" Jack asked.

"I'm ridin' with a fraternity brother, but there would probably be room for her. It's just the two of us," said Tobe.

"Why don't you come over for dinner Friday night, around six o'clock, and I'll invite her. You guys can talk about it."

"What does she look like?" Being twenty years old, Tobe was always on a female safari.

"She's a wild one from what I hear."

"What does she look like?"

"A real rebel, independent sort."

"What does she look like?"

"And really smart—"

"Okay, I get the picture."

"No. She's pretty cute, actually," Jack said.

"You're messing with me, my friend."

"I know she was valedictorian when she graduated from White Mountain High. And no, bro, I ain't messin' with you. She is attractive—"

"You better not be lying to me."

"In her own way."

"I'll see you Friday."

Tobe had actually heard, while he was playing football at the junior college, from a former teammate from White Mountain about the preacher's daughter there and had a great curiosity about her. It seemed quite fortuitous.

The last weekend of Christmas break began on Friday night at Jack and Shirley's apartment, before Tobe was to return to school on Sunday.

Tobe arrived early.

"Okay, Shirley, give it to me straight," Tobe said to Jack's wife after they were seated in their little living room. "What does this Anne Sternbridge look like?"

"Well," Shirley hesitantly began, "she's not what you would call beautiful—more what you would call an—interesting, or strong—face."

"She has a very nice smile," Jack said, "and pretty gray eyes. Besides, what difference does it make? You've got a girlfriend."

At that moment, there was a soft knock on the door, and Shirley went to answer. Tobe held his breath and thought about Bettyjean. *Jack's right. I've got a girlfriend.* And then he saw Anne Sternbridge. *Had a girlfriend,* he corrected himself.

"Sorry if I'm late," Anne said as she entered. "I had to deliver some groceries to this colored family on the other side of town. The church's yardman, actually."

What Tobe saw before him was a young lady about his age, twenty or so, a little on the smallish side, maybe five two, with short brown hair, fair skin, strong facial bone structure, and a petite figure. He noted too that her voice was soft, low, and sardonic. *No,* Tobe thought, *she's not beautiful, but there's something about her that charms me,* and he was totally intrigued.

"Anne Sternbridge, this is Tobe Stanhope," Jack said. "Tobe, Anne."

Tobe accepted Anne's proffered hand while noticing her unusual gray eyes.

"I've been wanting to meet you for a long time," Tobe said.

"How do you know about me?" Anne asked.

"I played football with Jim Long at Mars Hill. He told me about you."

"Oh, for God's sake. Don't you guys have more important things to talk about than some bimbo?" Anne said.

Tobe was uncertain about an answer and gave none.

"They pay our janitors starvation wages. These fine Baptist Christians." Tobe noted the sarcasm in her voice and liked it. "I've been conducting food drives while on Christmas break for our less fortunate colored brethren."

"That's very—"

"I'm also trying to get them registered to vote," Anne continued.

"You can't—"

"Oh yes I can. Unfortunately, I have to go back to school, but just wait till next summer. I'm going to get every colored person in this county registered."

Tobe feebly asked her if she needed a ride back to Meredith, and travel arrangements ensued.

"So what's your major?" Anne asked Tobe as they all four sat at the small dining table in Jack and Shirley's dwarfish kitchen.

"Philosophy," Tobe answered.

"And what are you going to do with that?"

"I haven't a clue." Tobe had no intention of revealing his plan to go to the seminary with his philosophy major and become a Baptist minister since he had now abandoned that career path.

"Ah, another Socrates. Just watch out for the hemlock," she cautioned, "and don't be corrupting the youth."

"And to make matters worse, I have a double minor in English literature and Latin."

"Are you serious?"

"Of course," Tobe said.

"Will you marry me?" she teased.

"I'll probably end up flipping hamburgers."

"But you can quote Keats while you're doing it, or Plato," she said.

"What's your major?" Tobe asked.

"English literature—and creative writing."

Perfect, Tobe thought while his eyes scanned her body. *Not bad,* in reference to it, *not in Bettyjean's class of course but ten times smarter.*

Anne went on to reveal a great deal about herself and her social conscious activities, such as organizing food drives for the homeless, visiting colored neighborhoods to register them to vote while learning their stories, giving blood by lying about her age, writing letters to the editor about various social and civic wrongs and injustices, and attending orphanages to read to parentless children. It became clear to Tobe during the course of the evening that Anne had a beautiful and caring soul, that she was precocious in word and deed, that she was innocent and sweet, and that, in Tobe's words, she was a "fucking genius." Tobe decided he was going to get to know her better.

"I didn't expect you to be so handsome," Anne said to Tobe as they were standing at the door, ready for departure. Tobe liked her directness and candor.

"And I didn't expect you to be so blind," Tobe said, trying feebly to be funny.

"I'll bet you're really vain," she said.

"Whoa, you don't pull any punches, do you?" Tobe realized that she didn't play games and always spoke her mind, candidness being her strong suit.

"Why should I?"

Tobe turned to his host. "Jack, am I vain?"

"I don't know. When we were roommates, you only spent two hours in front of the mirror every mornin'," Jack kidded.

"But I spent three times that much in the library."

"Tryin' to pick up women," Jack said.

"Our coeds? Are you kiddin'?"

"Wait a minute," Shirley said.

"That doesn't include you," Tobe clarified.

"It doesn't matter. You're not my type anyway," said Anne.

Is she putting me on or is she serious? Tobe wondered with a slightly achy feeling of rejection.

Then arrangements were finalized for Sunday's drive back to school, and good nights were tossed around while Tobe stared into space and thought of Shakespeare's *Troilus and Cressida*. "I am giddy; expectation whirls me round," Troilus said in anticipation of being with Cressida. "Th'imaginary relish is so sweet That it enchants my sense." *I just hope she doesn't act like Cressida, who said, "Men prize the thing ungained more than it is," while playing hard to get.*

The following Sunday, Tobe and his fraternity brother Ron pulled into the ESSO service station at the crossroads just outside of Belhaven, and Tobe noticed a sparkling black Cadillac Seville sitting off to the edge of the area with a back window open and Anne peering out.

"That's them over there," Tobe said, pointing. As they pulled up alongside the Cadillac, its trunk popped up, and three doors opened simultaneously as Anne and her parents exited the car.

Anne introduced her parents to Tobe, and Tobe introduced Ron to everyone. Tobe noted that Anne's father appeared lean, compact, and handsome; his demeanor was smooth, polished, and self-possessed; his language arrived with full articulation, rich in metaphor and vitality, with just a trace of the South. His appearance seemed crafted to perfection; he wore a silk dress shirt with a diamond stud adorning his silk tie, a suit that was perfectly tailored to hug his body without a wrinkle and bottomed off with sleek, brilliant shoes.

To Tobe, Mrs. Sternbridge seemed like a work of art. She was petite with lush amber hair, white skin, and a sweet face. Later in the car with Anne, Anne would tell him that her mother owned a wardrobe that would be the envy of the queen of England and that she dressed every day as though she were going to a wedding or a funeral, which often she was. Anne would tell Tobe that her mother had no jeans, no slacks, no work dresses, no work shoes, no sneakers, no flats, no aprons, no gardening clothes—nothing that was not frilly, girly, or coquettish—and that she had worn high heels shoes so often that the muscles in her calves had contracted such that she was unable to stand barefooted. To Tobe, she did not look like a Southern Baptist preacher's wife, nor apparently did she want to, although she seemed to play the part convincingly. It seemed to Tobe that her glamorousness could be misinterpreted as flirtatious, or as coyily girlish.

In Ron's small car, Tobe rode shotgun in the front seat while Anne lagged on the back seat. It was to be a three-hour drive, so Tobe saw it as a rich opportunity to gently query Anne, whom he was curious to get to know better.

"So what's your major?" Ron began.

If we can just get past Ron's inanities, Tobe thought. Tobe took the initiative and turned himself around in the front seat in order to half-face Anne a little better.

"I like your parents," Tobe said. "They seem really nice."

"Very," she said. She also seemed cautious and distant, which years later Tobe would come to understand.

"Your mother's a very attractive woman." Tobe sought her good graces.

"She knows. She's my main competition."

Tobe was undeterred. "Where did your dad get his doctor's degree?"

"New Orleans Baptist Theological Seminary."

"Deep South, huh? Are you from the South?"

"Georgia."

"How did you get to North Carolina?"

"White Mountain Baptist Church called my dad."

"I see."

"Where were you born?" She finally showed an interest.

"North Carolina. My mother is actually from South Carolina," he said.

"I hate, loathe, and despise the South," she said.

"Oh yeah?"

"Because I hate bigotry, prejudice, white supremacy, and all that shit."

"I just ignore it," Tobe mumbled.

"I think my dad's going to try to get out of the South, and I admire him for it."

"Well," Tobe said, "I certainly don't like all the hate talk."

"Let me tell you what happened to my dad while I was home on Christmas break. I was so mad I could—I could—arrrgh," Anne began.

"Go for it," Tobe encouraged her.

"I could have killed somebody, even though I don't believe in violence. We have a colored man who is the janitor of our church, and he and his family live in a cottage in back of the church," Anne said.

"Not the same as the yardman."

"No. Well, last weekend, a water pipe broke in one of the women's restrooms, and our janitor stayed up all Saturday night fixing it, finishing just before church started Sunday morning."

"Good man."

"Yes. He said to my dad, 'Well, I guess me and my family won't be able to make it in time for our church,' which is about twenty miles away," Anne explained.

"A colored church."

"Of course. 'Well,' my dad said, 'just go get your family and bring them here. You can sit in the balcony, if you're more comfortable that way.'"

"I can see what's coming."

"Yes. So that Sunday night, my dad got a phone call from the chairman of the board of deacons, wanting an appointment, along with two other deacons, with my dad. So, on Wednesday before prayer meeting, they showed their ugly, pathetic faces at my dad's office."

"And they said—"

"'Don't ever let this happen again.' Of course my dad explained the circumstances to them," Anne continued.

"Did they understand?"

"They said, 'Next thaing you know, they'll be braingin' their friends, and once you let 'em in, there's no stoppin' 'em. And then next thaing you know, they'll be wantin' to marry our daughters—'"

"That's so tiresome."

"And my dad said, 'Get out of my office.'"

"Good for him."

"And then they threatened him."

"Figures," Tobe said.

"And my dad said to me and my mother, 'I try to teach Jesus's message of love, and what do I get in return?'"

"Hate."

"My father's a very enlightened and benevolent man—and wise. I don't think he can endure this environment much longer. I think he's going to look for somewhere else to go," Anne concluded.

Through the remainder of the trip, Anne showed her sensitivity, extreme intelligence, and a broad range of knowledge, discoursing on everything from Nietzsche to Emily Dickinson, two of Tobe's favorite subjects. He had had a course in each of them and so could stay abreast of her. He was totally captivated.

As they were depositing Anne at her dorm on the campus of Meredith College, Tobe said, "Can I call you?"

Anne's Cressida-like reply was "We'll see," even though she did give Tobe her dorm phone number, which was an encouraging sign to Tobe.

It had been two weeks since they had driven together back to school for the beginning of the spring semester, which was now well under way. He thought he'd wait an indifferent span of time, not to seem too eager, before calling her, which he calculated was the present moment. He had thought about nothing but her since the ride back and had fought mightily to suppress his eagerness to talk to her.

"Anne?" Tobe said into the receiver.

"Yes?"

"This is Tobe."

"Who?"

"Aw, come on."

"No, seriously, Tobe who?" she said.

"How many Tobes do you know?"

"None," she answered.

Now he felt like an idiot.

"What a short memory you have. Or maybe I'm just forgettable, unlike Nat King Cole's 'Unforgettable,' which is 'what you are, in every way.'"

"Actually, I've been sitting by the phone night and day waiting for you to call," she said.

He was never certain what to make of her. He knew that she was brilliant, and yet sometimes she seemed so simple, so childlike. At times, she seemed naïve, unsophisticated, unadorned socially. *Is it naïveté or a sophisticated game?*

"How's the semester going?" he asked.

"Great! I'm into the Romantic poets and Shakespeare this semester—along with some other boring requirements."

"I'm taking a course in existentialism this semester. I think it's going to be my undoing," he said.

"Why is that?"

"I've been going through a sort of crisis lately."

"What kind of crisis?"

"Oh, you know, philosophical, theological, spiritual, that kind of thing."

"I can relate," she said.

"You can?"

"Absolutely."

"I think existentialism may win the battle."

"You've never mentioned this," she said.

"We haven't had a chance to talk about things—without a fraternity brother present."

"Tell me more."

"That's why I called. I thought we might get together next weekend and get to know each other better."

"I don't know. I've got a lot of studying to do." She reverted to her Cressida mind-set.

"Oh, well, in that case—"

"But I could take a little time off—like, say, Friday night," she said.

"You just saved my life."

"Do you know who Martin Luther King is?" Anne asked Tobe as they sat in the reception area of her women's dormitory at Meredith College on Friday night.

"Who?"

"Martin Luther King Jr."

"I know who Martin Luther is, but I don't think he was ever a king," Tobe said. "He nailed the ninety-five theses on the church door in Wittenberg. One of my heroes, actually."

"No, no, not him," Anne said.

"He went through a tremendous spiritual crisis and resolved it through a close study of the scriptures while cultivating his faith," Tobe went on.

"Have you heard of the Montgomery bus boycott?" Anne said, continuing on her path, parallel to his.

"Defied the pope, listened to his inner self, and started the whole Reformation movement." Tobe continued on his own lateral path, not intersecting with hers. "I wish I had his faith."

"How about Rosa Parks?" she said.

"Hey, I'm a student. I spend all my time with my nose buried in books in the library, trying to pass exams. I haven't seen a newspaper in weeks," he said, defending himself.

"You've got a hero. Well, she's my hero."

"I've heard the name," Tobe said.

"A simple woman who is changing the course of history."

"How so?"

"Well, started about a year ago. She was sitting at the front of a full bus when a white man got on the bus—this was in Montgomery, Alabama—and the bus driver told her to get up and give the man her seat."

"Common practice."

"And she said, 'No. I been workin' all day, and I'se tared,' and then she was arrested."

"Wow, some guts," Tobe said.

"And that's how it started. Made all the news. Martin Luther King, who is a preacher at a colored church in Montgomery, began to lead a boycott of the Montgomery bus system. Every colored person in Montgomery refused to ride the bus—helping each other out with carpools, bicycles, walking to work, whatever. After a year of enduring a great inconvenience for coloreds, the Supreme Court ruled that segregation on public transportation in Alabama was unconstitutional, and segregation on buses came to an end."

"That *is* history making," Tobe said.

"I want to be like her. What am I doing studying Keats when I could be doing something worthwhile?"

"Studying Keats is important too."

"I've been seriously thinking about going to Montgomery to join the cause."

"Don't do that. Take care of yourself first. You'll be more useful if you finish your education first," Tobe argued. He had developed a personal opinion about her whereabouts, of course, because he wanted her nearby.

"That's selfish. I think the time has come for justice for African Americans in the South."

"It'll never happen," Tobe said.

"You know what Rosa said? She said, 'The bus was among the first ways I realized there was a colored world and a white world.'"

"Welcome to my South," Tobe said.

"You know how Plato compared the human soul to a chariot drawn by two horses, one black and one white, the one always pulling downward, the other always pulling upward?"

"I know Plato, philosophy major that I am. He was talking about the dichotomy of the human soul."

"Well, fighting segregation is like that."

"I don't think that's what he had in mind," Tobe said, defending Plato.

"Okay. Follow me. You've got two horses, one's white, the other's black, and there are two riders, circus riders maybe, standing on each horse's back, and they're trying to dance with each other, but the horses are bouncing up and down and pulling away from each other and running at different speeds, and it's impossible for the two dancers to dance with each other as long as they're dancing on horses."

"That would be hard, yes," Tobe confirmed.

"So how are they going to be able to dance with each other under those circumstances?"

"I give up," Tobe said.

"Easy. All the dancers need to do is get off their high horses, black and white, and get down on level ground and dance in great harmony, where everything is even, where there are no black and white horses."

"Never happen," Tobe said.

"Okay, gentlemen, curfew time," the dorm mother said, a reminder that women retire at a decent hour and young men go home.

Spring Break, 1956

Tobe and Bettyjean had stayed in touch by lots of letters and a few telephone calls over the months that separated them, and they met on the rare occasions when Tobe could get home from school. While Bettyjean was as gorgeous as ever, having won several more beauty contests in the interim, Tobe deep inside felt a slippage, which he was very curious about and a little guilty over. How could any man not be madly in love with such a Venus de Milo when 99.9 percent of all males would give their right testicle to have a creature like her on their arm? True, Tobe was still extremely attracted to her physically, cherished her sweetness, and relished seeing her. But there were problems.

First, Bettyjean was determined to be a preacher's wife, and Tobe had moved out of that orbit, and, two, he was bored to tears in her presence and had basically outgrown her intellectually. Still, there was that pulchritude element that was hard to walk away from. His conversations with Bettyjean dulled in comparison to his intellectual stimulation with Anne.

He waffled, he debated, he committed to Bettyjean one minute and uncommitted the next. He lay awake at night, again, and took lots of walks in the greening spring. He would make an effort at trying to reconcile things with her, and so spring break, 1956, stole upon him. He drove to Spartanburg as soon as he could after coming home to Belhaven.

Bettyjean's house, a colonial style, triple-storied, redbrick, accentuated with white shutters, was located in a luxurious area of Spartanburg, with wide green lawns, colorful flower gardens, titan-sized old oaks, and variegated shrubbery. Tobe had been here before, for the after-church Sunday dinner, but he had been too dazzled by Bettyjean at the time to notice the house itself, and so he sat in her driveway for a few moments to take it all in and whistled softly. He thought of his parents' modest dwelling by comparison and felt intimidated.

Bettyjean answered the door.

"Hey" was followed by lots of hugging and kissing, and a rush came upon him again. How, he wondered, could he ever walk away from such passion? How indeed.

"It is so good to see you, to feel your presence and your delicious body and look into your face. All becomes right with the universe when I'm with you," Tobe confessed, shoving aside his doubts.

"Me too," she said.

That's it, Tobe thought. *I'm going to forget about Anne. Bettyjean and I are made for each other. I'll help make an intellectual out of her.*

"Have you ever heard of existentialism?" Tobe asked when they finally took a break from their passionate activities.

They were seated on a pink brocade, billowy couch in the Godwins' living room. The floor of the room was a wall-to-wall beige carpet and tastefully conjoined all the furnishings and décor, which consisted of lots of mahogany tables, brocaded wing chairs, crystal lamps, and multicolored, lush drapery. Tobe was comfortable amidst such refinement and glowed with aesthetic pleasure.

"What?" she said.

And so he began to try to explain some philosophical concepts aside from Christianity to her, at the end of which she said, "Do you like this color of lipstick?" Tobe despaired and yearned to talk to Anne. With Bettyjean, the only way he knew to fill the silent gaps was to hug and kiss, which was certainly pleasurable enough—but he vaguely sensed it was not going to be enough to make a life. And spring break mercifully ended.

Back in school, Tobe watched the spring semester deepen and welcomed the dogwoods, pansies, and benevolent skies. He grew ever more attached to Anne, to the point that he was transfixed by her brilliance, her sweet spirit, her eccentric ways, and unconventional thoughts, enthralled and enslaved as he was. They saw each other often, weekends mostly, and being penniless college students, their time together consisted of nature walks, the reception area of the women's dorm, free campus movies, studying, ostensibly, in the library, punctuated with numerous breaks, sitting on the lawn, holding hands under the gnarled, budding oaks— all activities accompanied by long, intense conversations about poetry, philosophy, social issues, and each other's innermost life. They grew close, and Anne ended her Cressida impersonation. As spring warmed, Tobe's fraternity decided that it would be a good time for a cookout and a keg party at the lake, with girlfriends included. Tobe invited Anne.

After hot dogs, hamburgers, and lots of beer, and after quietude had settled over the party, mainly due to palliative music and some slow dancing, Tobe and Anne sat on a log in front of the dying embers to hold each other. In the middle of a conversation about Nietzsche's theory of the Übermensch, the superman, Tobe suddenly turned to Anne with a question.

"Would you wear my pin?" he asked as he watched the light from the campfire dancing shadows across Anne's face.

"Pen?" Anne, looking deep into the fire, questioned. "I have a pen already."

"My Sigma Chi pin."

"Why would I wear your fraternity pin?" Anne continued staring into the campfire, seeming to Tobe to be barely on the edge of awareness. Tobe could never tell when Anne was being unworldly or a genius of deception. Perhaps it was a little of both.

"It's called being pinned," Tobe explained.

"As in being pinned down?"

"Well, you might say that. It's a very serious commitment."

"Does this happen very often?"

"A fraternity pin is not just a piece of jewelry. It's part of your identity, designating a loyalty to your brothers."

"You only have one brother."

"Members of the same fraternity are regarded as brothers, and your fraternity pin is a public declaration of your belief in the rules and principles of the fraternity and your commitment to your brothers. It's a sacred trust."

"Rules—like getting drunk every weekend?"

"Pinning your girlfriend is a tradition. Because a fraternity pin has such weighty significance, it implies a—well, it's the next thing to being engaged."

"Do you do the pinning?" she asked.

"Yes."

"Where?"

"Huh, on your, er, chest."

"I bet it's just an excuse to fondle your girlfriend."

"I'll let you put it on yourself," he offered.

"Am I your girlfriend?"

"That was my assumption."

Tobe felt it was the perfect moment to raise the question he had been wanting to ask for quite some time.

"The way I see it, Anne, life is too short to waste a moment playing games. When you find someone whom you know the universe has sent to you to be your soul mate, you commit. Life is over in the blink of an eye."

"It is brief, isn't it."

"Every tick of the clock is a moment lost to all eternity. I want to spend the rest of my moments with you."

Tobe received a loud silence as her response.

"'Time has, my lord, a wallet at his back wherein he puts alms for oblivion.' Ulysses, from Shakespeare's *Troilus and Cressida*," Tobe said.

"Leave it to Shakespeare."

"A great-sized monster of ingratitudes."

"You're going to make me sad," Anne said softly.

"I know your dad is a Baptist minister, but religion takes its origins in the tyranny of time, an honest attempt to evade the great nada," Tobe said.

He noticed that Anne had begun to unclasp her watch from her wrist and slowly slide it over her hand. While she picked up a rock and looked around for another one, Tobe ambled on philosophically without processing Anne's actions, absorbed in his own musings, until he saw her smashing her watch on a rock with another rock. He quickly curved back to awareness.

"What the—"

"I hate the whole concept of time. I want to destroy time," Anne passionately said, then stood up, walked to the campfire, and tossed the ruined watch into the fire.

Tobe was stupefied. Anne returned to the log on which they were sitting.

"That was an expensive-looking watch," Tobe said. "I was just admiring it this evening. You didn't have to do that."

"I hate time."

"Yeah. Don't we all. But you didn't change anything."

"Yes I did. I eradicated time—for me—from now on." She broke into a southern drawl. "I jest got shud uv it."

"Nice try."

"You can do the pinning if you want to," Anne offered.

"You'd let me?" Tobe looked down at the pin on his shirt and started fumbling with it, finally detaching it. He held it up and then became uncertain how to proceed.

"Go ahead," she encouraged him.

And he did, very slowly and cautiously lifting her sweater away from her body, sticking the pin carefully in and clasping it. He then kissed her very gently on her lips and said the only thing he knew to say, "I love you."

Toward the end of the spring semester, Anne wrote Tobe a long letter expressing her concern about what was transpiring in Alabama: Martin Luther King's home was fire bombed in Montgomery, and while Autherine Lucy, a colored coed, was admitted to the University of Alabama, riots on campus erupted, and she was sent home on the indefensible excuse that the university could not provide protection for her. Anne explained to Tobe that she had written Autherine a sympathetic letter and offered to try to get her admitted into Meredith College, for which she was immediately rebuffed by her own college after a confrontation with the dean of admissions. She told Tobe that she was appalled by her administration's attitude of aggressive indifference and that she suggested to Autherine that she, Anne, would travel to Alabama if it would help any.

Meanwhile Tobe was awestruck by the fact that Elvis had four straight number-one hits that spring, "Don't Be Cruel," "Hound Dog," "Heartbreak Hotel," and "Blue Suede Shoes," all of which, even on a starvation budget, Tobe added to his collection. He and Elvis had been born in the same year, in the South, into poverty and fundamentalism and Baptist hymns and gospel songs, which Elvis converted to magical music but which stifled Tobe's soul.

That spring, while things were starting to heat up in southern colored-white relationships, Eden descended on Tobe and Anne's relationship, and they stayed in constant contact with each other either by phone or letters. Tobe told her how excited he was about his encounter with existentialism, how it gave him some solid footing and confidence in his personal groping toward the light, how it warmed his spiritual fires and caused him to live with his religious apostasy ever more comfortably. Meanwhile, Anne wrote to Tobe about her encounters with Wordsworth, Coleridge, Keats, Shelley, Byron et al. and shared with Tobe those who ignited her soul. She was especially drawn to Blake's mysticism. *I thought she would be,* Tobe mused, himself finding Blake, who often saw spiritual creatures outside his window, mysteriously spiritual. They lived together in their own little eternity in their shared hours, but Anne told Tobe that she was not completely contented because of the growing shadow of the monster of discontentment that was segregation among many southern coloreds across the South, culminating with the rejection of seven colored students to a public school in Kentucky. She communicated to Tobe that she felt superfluous and wanted to do something but was unsure what to do. Little Rock, Arkansas, the first assault on segregation, had receded into the far past. Tobe sympathized but coaxed her into acceptance of southern reality, temporarily. And the spring semester ended.

Summer plans were amorphous for both. Tobe thought he would go back to his hometown of Belhaven to see if he could find some type of summer job, while Anne dreamed of studying in England, for which she had already accumulated information and applications. They vowed to write letters frequently and feverishly.

Back in Belhaven, Tobe fell into a job as a lifeguard, for which he was supremely unqualified. During the second week of employment at the swimming pool, he was visited at his home one Sunday afternoon by several deacons from East Belhaven Baptist with a proposition. "Seein's as how you declared yourself for the ministry and seein's how you're a ministerial student up there at that there college, you might want to git some experience by serving as the summer student minister of our little Baptist mission in Browntown." It was apply named, Tobe supposed, not because of the color of people's skin but by the grime that colored the neighborhood. It was actually named after the original family, the Adam Browns.

"I don't know," Tobe responded. "I think I'll have to pray about it. That's a heavy undertaking."

"Sho' is," agreed the deacon spokesman. "Take yo' time—but we'd like to make some type of announcement at Wednesday night's prayer meetin'."

"I don't know if God will speak that soon, but I'll do some serious praying and listening," Tobe said.

"Give me a call by to'mara," the spokesman said as he walked out the Stanhopes' front door.

Tobe would indeed do some serious praying, not about what God wanted him to do but about how he was going to tell them no.

"Sounds like a great opportunity," his father said as they sat down to Sunday supper.

"Yeah, I suppose," Tobe reluctantly agreed.

"Give you some great experience, help you make some money—I'll even help you with a car," his father said.

"I'm going to tell them no."

"This'd give you a chance to see if'n it's what God wants you to do," his father said.

"I just can't do it."

"I don't git it."

"I cannot get up there in front of those poor people every Sunday, looking into the eyes of those upturned faces, and lie to them," he said, bravely fortifying his position.

"Lie? What the hell you talkin' 'bout?" His father turned red. "You stood up in front of the congregation of East Belhaven Baptist Church and announced that God had called you to be a preacher. Now whatta you gonna tell 'em?"

"I'm not going to tell them anything. Besides, God wants me to be a teacher," he mumbled.

"What am I gonna tell 'em? I have to face 'em every Sunday. I'm the superintendent of Sunday school, on the board of deacons, a leader in the church."

"They're not going to fire you," Tobe said.

"You're tryin' to humiliate me, that's what you tryin' to do."

"Tell them your son's crazy, tell them your son's an idiot, tell them your son's going straight to hell, tell them anything you want to, I don't give a damn!" He stood and swatted his napkin on the table and withdrew his presence from the room.

"Don't you use that kinda language in my house, ya hear me!" The father then spooned out another plate of pinto beans and forked another pork chop.

Tobe heard his father mumble something about "Wonder what he meant by 'lie to them.'"

Meanwhile, Anne flew off to England to spend six weeks studying English literature at Oxford. Through her letters, Tobe received the impression that it was a blessed summer for her, and he envied her.

Tobe read her words to himself:

> Dearest Tobe: I have arrived safely, and all is well. The Oxford countryside is stunningly peaceful, with high green hills, tranquilly grazing sheep, dense woods, numerous noisy creeks and streams, fabulous skies, and

slowly moving farmers—ah, and the smell of new-mown hay is always in the air. In England in the summer, it does not get dark until almost midnight. One just wants to run and play outside eternally.

I have a roommate whose name is Sheila Lincoln, and she is colored, and she is from Birmingham, Alabama, and she is beautiful. We have already had long, soul-baring talks, and it is heartbreaking. Although I have lived in the South all my life, a white South, she is ushering me into her world, a world composed of being Negro and living in the segregated South. She is a sweet human being, but she is angry, and if she is any indicator, there is anger seething below the surface among southern coloreds, and I don't think it can be contained forever. Oh, Tobe, I tremble at the thought of what is going to happen, and I don't think it will take much to light the fuse on this atomic bomb. It will probably take a leader—whoever it may be—to channel their anger.

I must tell you that Sheila is too gorgeous for words. She is so smart, so sweet, and so beautiful that I think I am falling in love. I don't know if I can trust myself around her, but I guess when I am tempted, I'll just think of you. Such strange sensations. Sheila wants to enroll in the University of Alabama in the fall. What bravery! I tell her it is hopeless, but she is determined. She is very conscious of what she is doing and of the significance of it all.

Well, tomorrow is the first day of class, so I've got to get in bed for now. I look forward to hearing from you and all about lifeguarding. Love you, Anne.

So Tobe's days were filled with hours around the swimming pool. It was an annoyingly boring job and a lonely one, whatever one might think about the image of a lifeguard. And Tobe cheated on the job. He brought tiny pieces of paper with poems written on them and spent much of his time on the umbrella-covered lifeguard chair while his eyes scanned the water, memorizing poetry. He was determined to make his time count and keep his mind active by enriching it. That was a big plus for his summer. He also turned extremely brown that summer.

Meanwhile, Bettyjean, whose grandmother lived in Charlotte, came up to visit her granny off and on throughout the summer, which provided Tobe and Bettyjean with many hours at the drive-in movies where some very perilous kissing and hugging took place on many a pleasant, still summer night. Tobe was still ripped apart by the vacillation of his feelings between her and Anne. In one way, he felt abandoned by Anne and adored by Bettyjean. He was also cognizant of the fact that he was betraying Anne and thought, *Oh well, that's what guys do when they feel deserted.*

On the other hand, he eventually discovered that any efforts he made at intellectualizing Bettyjean were futile. She was a smart enough girl, but she was not interested in ideas. She had potent maternal instincts and sought, above all else, to become a mother and preacher's wife, not necessarily in that order. In addition, she announced one day that she had been accepted into Tobe's university, Wake Forest, for the following fall. Tobe made a soft gulping sound. Bettyjean's reality was forcing itself upon him and, sooner or later, would have to be dealt with.

One evening in August, exhausted and aroused from a lengthy session of physicality and a murderous suppression of the libido with Bettyjean, Tobe sat up to take a break and catch his breath. Tobe always felt that the reason they engaged in "lovemaking" so much was because they had so very little to say to each other. Conversation was difficult.

"Bettyjean," he began, "I want to ask you a question."

"Okay."

"How would you feel about—instead of being a preacher's wife—being the wife of a college professor?"

"I don't know any college professors."

"You're looking at one," he said.

"What?"

"I think so."

"I don't know what you're talking about."

"I've been through hell and back again," Tobe said.

"How?"

"I've tried to imagine myself living the life of a Baptist preacher. Let me just put it this way: I would either die of a heart attack from the pain of hypocrisy, kill myself, or merely disappear one day never to be heard from again."

"Why?"

She's such a great conversationalist, Tobe thought sarcastically.

"How could I devote myself to God and try to convince others about Him when I'm not even sure myself—about—about God," he said, but the truth materialized before him. *There's no way she can understand the turmoil and torture I've been through. Her faith is so unquestioning and simple. She makes me feel obscene—like I'm of Satan's party.*

"Whatever you want to do, Tobe, is ... fine ... with ... me," she said as her voice faded to a whisper.

"Sure it is," Tobe softly responded.

As a lifeguard, Tobe had a lot of temptations that summer, which he had little willpower to resist. Bettyjean came up to Charlotte only once in a while, and the rest of the time, Tobe was free to roam, which he did. He was not an experienced sexual partner when the summer began, but he fell into the hands of a married lady, Charlene, whose husband was a truck driver and was out of town most of the time.

Charlene was able to escort Tobe through the intricacies of the sexual dance, and Tobe proved to be a fast learner and was soon teaching her a few tricks (he had lots of dirty books hidden in his bedroom, behind his Bible and Sunday school literature, which served as his instructional manual and his user's guide). To Tobe, she seemed responsive and excited by some of the things he showed her, and he grew to a better understanding of himself. If he really cared about Bettyjean, he pondered, he would not be doing the things he was doing with Charlene, but he also knew that he would never touch Bettyjean in that way unless they were married. And Anne was an Atlantic Ocean away. It was all such undiscovered country for him, and there were others besides Charlene of course. Tobe also came to the sober realization that Bettyjean did not know what he was really like—and he was just beginning to acknowledge his true nature. *I may seem like a scoundrel to some people,* he thought, *but I've hardly experience life yet.* This feeling applied mostly to Bettyjean, from which Anne was exempted.

He began to like the lifeguarding job better before the summer was over. It had many perks. He also silently resented Anne's independence and distance.

Fall Semester, 1956

"Well, I think me and Shirley are going to hit the ole hay for right now." Jack Workman's mouth quivered as he seemed to try to stifle a yawn. "We're gonna leave the evenin' to you two."

Tobe and Anne, who had taken a long weekend break from their studies to visit Tobe's ole buddy, sat at the small Formica-topped table in Jack and Shirley's Lilliputian kitchen. Tobe had asked Jack earlier if he and Anne could come for a little getaway respite—and to use their sleeper sofa for a night or two. Tobe knew that Jack would understand what he had on his mind, Jack knowing Tobe's mind very well, and that Jack and Shirley would give them all the privacy they needed, even in a one-bedroom apartment.

"Thanks for dinner, Shirley," Tobe said as Shirley was putting the last items in the kitchen cabinets. "It was delicious."

"Okay," Shirley said, turning to go, "now you two behavior yourselves."

"Right," Tobe mumbled.

"Me and Jack are heavy sleepers," Shirley added on her way out, "so you can make all the noise you want to."

"I promise not to watch," Jack whispered as he departed for their bedroom.

"Watch what?" Anne asked.

"I haven't the faintest," Tobe lied. Tobe had never really explained to Anne why he wanted to go visit his old buddy, aside from telling her he wanted to spend some time with her away from dorm mothers, college campuses, and libraries, somewhere they could have some time, closeness, and privacy—and be really intimate—he intimated. He was not sure whether Anne had read the subtext.

"Not a lot of room," Jack had told Tobe on the phone, "but you're welcome to use the sleeper sofa in the living room."

"That's all I need—just a bed." Tobe smiled.

It was Tobe's senior year in college, and Anne was in her junior year, in the fall of 1956, and they had been seeing each other since the last winter's break, even though Anne had been in England for a large portion of the summer. To make matters worse, Tobe's university had moved to the town of Winston-Salem where the RJ Reynolds Tobacco Company had built Wake Forest an elegant, Georgian-style new campus, a hundred miles away from Anne's campus in Raleigh. Frequent visits had become infrequent.

Tobe had never asked Anne about her virginal status, but he assumed that since they were now officially pinned, nature would be allowed to take its course, and even though he had not directly addressed the issue of why exactly they had gone to visit Jack and Shirley, he also assumed that Anne sensed what was going on and what he had on his mind, being a healthy twenty-one-year-old male. On the other end, he had become estranged from Bettyjean, due in large part to his philandering as a lifeguard during the summer. As far as he was concerned, commitment had occurred between him and Anne, and there was no longer any need for them to hold back. He was totally bedazzled by his devotion to Anne. What Tobe felt guilty about, feeling less than honest, was that he had let neither Bettyjean nor Anne know about the other, but his friend Jack forgave him anyway.

"Well, shall we move to the living room?" Tobe asked Anne as he stood up. To call it a living room was a delusional misnomer. Jack and Shirley's apartment consisted of a galley kitchen, everything within reach by standing in the middle of it, with a smallish dining table by the door, one master (more delusion) bedroom. The "living" area (delusion) had a couch and coffee table in front of the windows, a front door entrance, an armchair to the left of the coffee table, and a small television on top of a smallish table across from the couch.

"Nietzsche or Dickinson?" Anne asked as she thumbed through some books on the coffee table.

"Nietzsche is too heavy for tonight—and definitely not very romantic," Tobe said. "I think Emily is just the right mood for this occasion."

"Yeah, I love Emily Dickinson," Anne said.

"I love her too."

"No, no. You don't understand," Anne said. "I don't just *love* Emily

Dickinson, I am *in* love with her, totally in love with her. Were she alive, I'd marry her."

"She'd be kind of old," Tobe said, laughing and feeling baffled. It was not the first time that Anne had made such a strange, seemingly sincere profession. In fact, Tobe expected such remarks and found them to be part of her unorthodox, quirky approach to life—and relationships.

"Listen," Anne said as she cleared her throat.

"Elysium is as far as to

The very nearest room,

If in that room a friend awaits

Felicity or doom.

What fortitude the soul contains

That it can so endure

The accent of a coming foot,

The opening of a door."

Silence prevailed. Finally, Tobe said, "Wow."

"Yeah. No expression of feeling. Not one. And no self-indulgence. And yet so powerful in its emotional conveyance."

"Just concrete images," Tobe added.

Tobe was gazing blindly at nothing, looking into the eyes of space, what little there was in Jack's apartment, when he heard the sound of paper being torn.

His eyes sidled toward Anne sitting next to him. She was meticulously tearing Dickinson's poem from the textbook.

"You shouldn't tear up books," Tobe said as he incredulously watched.

"It's for a good cause," Anne whispered as she lifted the poem with both hands high in the air above her head like a priestess in some type of sacred ritual. Silence followed and then: "Now. Bless this poem to the nourishment of my soul, and my soul to the service of poetry, in the name of the universe," Anne said softly. She brought the piece of paper down, kissed it, put the piece of paper in her mouth, and began to chew.

"What the—" Tobe caught himself. He had been trying not to let the bizarre things Anne did surprise him, so he decided to try to cover his shock with humor. "Didn't you have enough dinner?" he asked with a wry face.

"Transubstantiation," Anne explained.

"Transubsta—"

"The Eucharist."

"Would you like some water?"

"A way of taking Emily Dickinson into my body since she's not here. Now she is mine." With that, Anne began to unbutton her blouse.

Tobe watched in confusion. He thought at first that perhaps she was feeling a little warm and was trying to cool off, but after she had finished the numerous buttons, she began to take first one arm out of her blouse and then the other one and then proceeded to take the blouse off completely. She slipped her shoes off, and Tobe began to get the point, so guilelessly.

"Let me get the lights," Tobe said as he went about dimming the room but leaving the light on in the kitchen.

Anne was standing by the couch unzipping her pants, which she then let fall to the floor, and within the beat of a pulse, her panties and bra (not that she needed one) had vanished.

"Wait a minute, wait a minute, whoa, slow down," Tobe said as he approached the couch.

"Problem?"

"Yeah, there is," he explained. "This is not the way things are done."

"Doesn't it start with taking off our clothes?"

"No. Yes. Eventually."

"Why waste time?"

"Making out is not wasting time."

"What?"

"It starts with kissing and hugging and holding close and giving pleasure until arousal sets in. *Then* slowly the clothes start coming off, little by little, mutually, and builds to a crescendo."

Silence.

"I don't think I can do that," Anne said.

"What?"

"I don't think I can do that."

"Kiss?"

"Yes."

"But we've kissed before."

"With no expectations."

More silence.

"I've fucked things up, haven't I?" she said.

"No, no, sweetie, not at all. I'm glad you have no experience. Let me take my clothes off and join you. But there's no rush, no pressure," Tobe said.

Tobe converted the sofa into a bed, unfurled some sheets to put on it, tossed on a couple of pillows Jack had provided, took his clothes off, and slid between the sheets. Anne followed him. She lay flat on her back staring at the ceiling while Tobe turned on his side in order to be able to kiss and touch her.

"I want you to know how much I love you—with all my heart," Tobe whispered close to her ear. Silence. "Don't you have anything to say?"

"No."

"I long for the day when we can get married and spend our lives together," Tobe said softly.

"Married?"

"Yeah, you know, church, preacher, wedding rings—"

"My daddy's a preacher."

"Yeah, I know that. Commitment, eternal happiness. Making love anytime we want to."

"Yuck."

"What?"

"Nothing."

He started kissing her cheek, her neck, her shoulder while his hand moved around over the terrain of her skinny body. As he tried to move his hand down to the jointure of her legs, he realized that she was covering her vagina with both her hands.

"Come on now, let's move your hands away from down there," he said as he pulled her hands away, a motion that was repeated several times. Her hands moved so swiftly back to cover her vagina that it was like her arms had a spring in them. Tobe moved his body as close as possible to her body, body touching body, and began kissing her on the lips. His strategy was to try to get her warmed up to the idea of their naked bodies being intertwined and to arouse some physical excitement in her. She seemed like a mrble statue that had fallen backward.

His hand moved gently down her belly, rubbing her softly as he worked his way down. Her flesh excited him, and he began to respond with an erection. "Touch me," he whispered.

"I can't."

"Why?"

"I don't like male genitalia."

"You don't like ma—"

"Let's talk about something else," she said.

"How about we don't talk at all."

By the time his hand reached her pubic hair, he realized that she had crossed her legs, and as he tried to slide his hand between her crossed thighs in order to pry them apart, they resisted. He went back to kissing her, first on the lips, then her chest, and then her breasts. He felt her quiver.

"Look," he said, "we don't have to do this."

"Just give me some time."

"We have all night. Let's just hold each other close and kiss and enjoy the feel of each other's body," he said. And so they did, for a long time, while Tobe thought, *There's something not quite right about this. I wish I knew what was going on.*

"Do you know the song, 'When Sunny Gets Blue?'" Tobe was relieved that she was finally able to form a sentence.

"Nat King Cole."

"It always reminds me of my roommate Chrissie. She has these gorgeous blue eyes, and she's very sensitive, and her eyes tear up a lot. She's so beautiful when she does that. I call her Sunny sometimes," Anne explained.

Why are we talking about her frigging roommate at a time like this? Tobe wondered.

Anne began to sing softly,

"When Sunny gets blue, her eyes get gray and cloudy,

Then the rain begins to fall, pitter-patter, pitter-patter,

Love is gone, so what can matter,

No sweet lover man comes to call."

"Nice," mumbled Tobe.

"Would you like to hear more?" Anne asked softly.

"I've got other things on my mind right now. Aren't you getting tired of being in that position? You're going to cut off the circulation to your legs," Tobe said. "Then gangrene will set in, and then your legs will have to be amputated." She uncrossed her legs while he spread them farther apart and rolled over on top of her. He was still erect and could feel that his penis was touching her.

"I'm going to try to come inside of you. Is that okay with you?"

"I guess so."

He could tell that every muscle in her body was as rigid as a steel cable, especially around her groin area. He made sure that everything was in the right place and then began to slowly push with his hips. No entry. He pushed again with the same results. He could tell that she was very small, but that was only part of the problem. It was like she was stiffening every muscle in her body, and, he knew, in her present tense condition, he would never gain entrance.

"I think you're purposely tightening your muscles. You need to relax."

"I don't know how," she said.

"Are you sure you want this to happen?"

"Yes."

In spite of his experiences of the previous summer as a lifeguard, he had never encountered a situation like this. The women he had known were forthcoming, so to speak, and required virtually no effort, expertise, or technical knowledge. It had been so easy, and he had no resources in his bank account of experience to make a withdrawal on in the present situation. Had he, he would have known that there were things one could do in this kind of situation, but he had lost his own virginity relatively late, being college age, and this was the fifties before the sexual revolution of the sixties. In the present situation, all he could do was see the ludicrousness of it all.

"Okay, Anne," he said, still lying on top of her, "let's give it one more try. Take a very deep breath and try as hard as you can to relax your whole body—and your mind too."

"Is sex supposed to be fun?" Anne asked.

"Very."

"What's the fun part? I can't breathe because you're lying on top of me, my leg muscles are hurting from being stretched apart, I can't move my arm, my head is pushing against the arm of the couch, and now you're trying to stab me to death. Tell me when the fun begins."

"All right, now," Tobe said, "we're going to give it one last try. Just relax and let me see what I can do." Tobe slowly and futilely started moving forward again, a centimeter at a time.

"Ow, ow, ow," Anne howled out in pain.

"Shhhh."

"You're hurting me."

"I'm not inside yet."

"You're too big. You're killing me," Anne complained.

"I guess I should be flattered," Tobe said, "but I know that I'm just average size."

"There's no way you're going to get all of that thing inside me. No way."

"I love you too much to hurt you," Tobe said.

"At least women don't hurt each other."

"What?" Tobe asked.

"Nothing."

"What did you mean by that?"

"I said nothing."

"Maybe some other time," Tobe said as he rolled off of her body and settled down beside her. "Let's just enjoy being close."

"I'm sorry."

"No, no. It's okay. We're just going to have to work on helping you relax. We're going to remove sex from the equation and practice being nude together while you practice relaxing."

"That sounds okay."

More silence.

"I do love you very, very much," Anne said softly from beneath the sheet.

"That makes me feel so warm all over," Tobe replied. "You already know how I feel." And they fell asleep.

Tobe returned to campus on Sunday evening in a state of great confusion, depression, and curiosity. Once on campus, he went to the library, which was the quietest place he could find to think about what had just happened that weekend, and found an empty carrel to sequester himself in. A return to his room, his roommate, and his frat brothers was out of the question. His roommate knew what he was going to do before the weekend started and would of course demand a descriptive re-creation of what happened, which would of course be punctuated by his roommate's running commentary, sarcasm, and off-color humor (a nice guy but still a guy). One of the purposes of the male sexual conquest of a woman is to perform the fraternal ritual of giving to his friends a vivid, detailed, and exaggerated account of exactly what happened; the truth of the matter is that there was usually less sex than was bragged about. That guy ritual he was not up to and sought the solitude of and retreat into the library.

He was confused by the fact that Anne did not seem to be very interested in having sex with him, that she never seemed to be aroused by all the kissing and touching and actually displayed no response or desire at all. He was depressed by the fact that he had so anticipated union with this person with whom he was insanely in love and knew in his soul that it would be otherworldly. Part of his depression also arose from the sheer disappointment of being unable to achieve that which he had wanted so badly. And then there arose curiosity about, or sheer puzzlement over, Anne's seeming indifference to sex with him and her bizarre comments and actions.

Something deep inside his brain hazed him, but he ignored it. He held fast to his feelings for her and denied all other possibilities. He was having an extremely difficult time classifying and sorting out what had happened.

After about an hour of tumbling with his thoughts, he decided, without having accomplished anything, including studying for the next day, that he needed sleep. Nothing had been resolved, nor could it be without first discussing these issues with Anne herself, because he was reluctant to admit the inadmissible.

He suddenly had a great urge to connect with Anne and pulled out a sheet of notebook paper from his book bag.

> Dearest Anne, there are so many things that I want to
> say to you, but the main thing is that I love you so very
> much—like I have never loved anybody in my life. I also

want you to know that our attempt at sex was not a frivolous, male ego escapade on my part but a deeply felt need to express the beauty of my feelings for you. It came from my soul, not my body. I know it seemed like a nightmare to you, and maybe that is my fault, and it did not work out the first time, but we are going to be patient and learn to do this together so that someday I know it will be the most beautiful thing we've either one experienced. I know our love and our closeness and affection will just grow and grow and become the most beautiful love affair in the history of the human race. I shall always love you, forever and ever. Tobe

He mailed it the next day.

As he was exiting his cubicle, he heard a voice whisper harshly to him, "Tobe." He turned to seen Gail, the redheaded art major from New Jersey, sitting at a study table. He sauntered over to her and sat down.

"I've been looking for you all weekend," she said.

"You have?"

"Where have you been?"

"I went home," he lied, except he had been in his home county with his friends Jack and Shirley.

"Oh."

"Why were you looking for me?" Tobe asked.

"I thought we might have some fun together."

"What kind of fun?"

"Oh, you know, a movie, dinner, maybe a hotel room." She winked at him, leaving no doubt what kind of fun she was talking about.

"How about next weekend?" Tobe said.

"It's a date."

Tobe left her table with promises and goodbyes, thinking, *Just what I need: a diversion.* He departed from the library with a possible solution on the horizon and a feeling of retribution for Anne's lack of cooperation. The male ego is a treacherous entity.

"I'm a virgin," Gail admitted as she was sitting on the edge of the bed while Tobe was sitting in the easy chair next to the bed in a room in the Salem Hotel on the following Friday night. They were now in downtown Winston-Salem, the economic capital of the North Carolina tobacco industry, to whose new campus, built by tobacco money (just as Duke had been), his university had now moved. Gail added, "But I'm tired of being one. I want to lose my virginity, and I want you to be the one to take it."

"I'm flattered," Toby answered honestly. "I just want you to know that I'm not all that experienced myself, but I think it would be fun to go through this together."

"Why don't you come sit by me on the bed," Gail said, patting a spot next to her.

"Good plan," Tobe said as he stood and moved toward her. He stood in front of her, looking down at her, then bent over to kiss her while she started touching his crotch. Tobe began to become excited as Gail did too.

"We're going to just take this real slow and let nature take its course," Tobe said as he began unbuttoning his shirt. Gail started unbuckling his belt.

"You seem awfully experienced to me," Tobe whispered as he slipped off his shoes while she pulled her sweater over her head to remove it. And so they proceeded to disrobe. Tobe's fingers trembled slightly with the rush of adrenaline and testosterone while Gail folded her arms across her breasts.

"Let me look at you," Tobe said. She dropped her arms and stood. Her skin was extremely white, her nipples rosy pink, and her pubic hair was as red as her head hair. She contrasted with Tobe's fading tan. Tobe pulled the covers back on the bed, and they separated the sheets with their bodies.

After the blood, the pain, and the awkwardness, they crossed the threshold of newness and settled into some passionate lovemaking for the rest of the weekend. In fact, they spent Friday night, all day Saturday, and Sunday morning repeating their merger as often as they could, taking breaks now and then for room service and some nourishment. And they talked and laughed and teased and came to know each other better.

As an art major, Gail was not exactly an Einstein, but she was a willing participant in something that Tobe needed badly—and she had a feathery touch. After his first night experience with Anne, he had begun to doubt himself because it had all been such a miserable failure. He had wondered if there was something wrong with him and his abilities at lovemaking. Gail was the antidote that he craved. After the weekend, he was assured that there was nothing wrong with him, having encountered his second virgin in two weeks, and could only come to the obvious conclusion that there must be something wrong with Anne.

But what? he wondered. *What could be the problem with her? I just don't get it.* He saw the irony in the fact that he really had no emotional attachment to Gail and yet they made out like a couple of lascivious college students, which they were, experiencing the thrill of an exciting new journey, while he idolized Anne and was not even able to penetrate her, much less make mad, passionate love to her. It was an enigma on which he would dwell for a while.

Meanwhile, Bettyjean had enrolled in the same university with Tobe, and Tobe witnessed her emergence as an instant magnet for all kinds of attention from every side because of her beauty and talent, becoming in time the most popular freshman on campus. She told him how she was asked to play the piano for many different occasions: the Rotary Club, the campus church, music department recitals, and any number of other civic organizations. To Tobe's chagrin, her beauty was heralded as well, and before the year was out, she had won the Miss Winston-Salem beauty contest.

Tobe knew that Bettyjean's choice of universities was based solely on her determination to be closer to him and with the hope that, being in close proximity to each other, they would develop into a real relationship. After all, they had never actually lived in the same town with each other, their relationship mostly made up of absence from each other. She told Tobe that her hope was that they could develop presence.

And Tobe's reaction? He hardly recognized her existence, although as the fall passed and her popularity grew, he began to have second thoughts about the situation and to have more long dialogues with himself, the chief question being,

What is wrong with me? Here the prettiest girl on campus has come to this school to be close to me, and I can't seem to bring myself to encourage the relationship. He thought about this long, hard, and often and came up empty, deciding that such is the enigma of chemistry and the human psyche. One night, he decided to make a phone call.

"Bettyjean?" Tobe said into the phone.

"Yes?"

"This is Tobe."

"Hi, Tobe. I didn't think you knew I existed." Sweetness incarnate was Bettyjean.

"I'm sorry. I've been really busy with studies and all. I spend a lot of time in the library." *And the Salem Hotel,* he thought.

"I've been busy too." She came across as nonchalant to Tobe.

"Including the Miss Winston-Salem beauty pageant."

"What do you want, Tobe?" Bettyjean said. Her sweetness had turned sour.

"Well, okay—look—I know. I mean, I'm sorry. I really have been studying a lot, and I know I've probably offended you."

"Probably? Yeah, probably."

"Well, I wanted to make it up to you." Tobe felt embarrassed.

"How?"

"Well, this weekend is the last football game of the season, and after the game, Sigma Chi is going to have a big bash, and I wanted to know if you'd like to go with me to the game and the party."

A long silence ensued.

"Bettyjean?"

"Yes?"

"Are you still there?"

"I'm here."

"Whatta you think?"

"Can I ask you a question?"

"Sure," he said.

"Is there going to be drinking at the party?"

Tobe was momentarily reeled. The subject had never come up before. "Is the pope Catholic?" he said.

"Are you going to drink?" Bettyjean asked.

"I'll probably imbibe a little." Tobe knew in his heart that he would have more than a little. His fraternity was notorious for its drinking.

"Do you remember what my father looked like when he came home for Sunday dinner—that time?"

"So?"

"My mother is a good Christian woman, just as I am, and she has had to tolerate that kind of thing her whole life. I am not going to live like that," she said.

"It's no big—"

"You are going straight to hell, Tobe Stanhope. Have a good life." Tobe was left holding the dial tone in his hand.

"I guess her answer is no," Tobe mumbled as he hung up the receiver.

Tobe returned to his carrel in the library to ponder what had just happened. *It's just as well,* he thought. *Try as I may, I cannot respond to Bettyjean, and the reason is I'm still in love with Anne, and no amount of Bettyjean's beauty can squelch that feeling I have for Anne. I must follow my heart. Besides, I cannot be a Baptist minister, and Bettyjean has her heart set on being a preacher's wife so she can be the church's pianist, regardless of what she says. She'll have no trouble finding a preacher who'll take her.* He picked up the poetry anthology for his American lit class lying on his desk in the carrel, and it fell open to Robert Frost:

> I shall be telling this with a sigh
> Somewhere ages and ages hence:
> Two roads diverged in a wood, and I—
> I took the one less traveled by,
> And that has made all the difference.

And then, on the next page, "But I am done with apple-picking now."

You are a beautiful, sweet, precious young lady, Bettyjean, and I'll miss you. But—goodbye. And Tobe learned a lesson in heart listening, no matter how stupid a decision may appear to the world.

"Anne?" Tobe said into the phone. "This is Tobe."

"Who?"

"Aw, come on, Anne. Don't do that."

"Oh, yeah, I remember you," she teased.

"Anne, my darling, I need to talk to you. I'm in great pain, and I need to try to get some relief from it."

"I'm sorry," she said.

"Can I come see you next weekend—please?"

"Well, I've got a big paper due—"

"Pleeeease," he begged.

"I'll try."

"You'll make me the happiest man in North Carolina if I can see you—and talk to you. I love you with all my heart."

"And I love you," she said.

"Do you?" He needed reassurance after his destiny-setting decision. He had learned that the heart has reasons of its own.

"Yes," she said simply.

"I'll get there either Friday night or Saturday morning—depending on how my car is running," he said, but he knew in his heart that a mere means of transportation would not stop him, although distance had become a problem for them this academic year.

As he hung up, he grew swirly again and remembered Troilus: "a joy too fine." It felt like getting an A on an exam or being admitted to Phi Beta Kappa or being named valedictorian. Friday could not come fast enough.

Tobe's last class on Friday, a philosophy seminar in which he had to write his senior thesis on a survey of modern (twentieth-century, that is) philosophy, ended at four in the afternoon. He returned, intellectually stimulated and elated at the weekend's prospects, to his room in his fraternity's living quarters in a wing of the men's dorms. His roommate was snoozing, either recovering from a week of studying or storing up resources for the weekend frat party, which Tobe would miss, which he cared not a gnat's eyelash for. He did not want to share with his roommate his weekend plans since he was in limbo about how his weekend would go, although he remained optimistic and hopeful.

As he was placing some toiletries and a change of clothes in his bag his room mate gained consciousness; Tobe warned him to be careful at the postgame bash and bade him adieu. His roommate was a good man and even a pre-ministerial student (as many of his most rowdy, partying fraternity brothers were, getting it out of their system before launching into the seminary—Baptist ministerial students being no different from priests in training—both very human).

The drive across mid-North Carolina from Winston-Salem to Raleigh in late fall through many small towns and villages was an exhilarating odyssey. The air was chilled, the sun autumn warm, the trees bare and stark with their geometrical patterns of irregularly shaped limbs (*Trees are more interesting without leaves,* he thought); the landscape provided rushing brooks, placid lakes, and deep woods with leafy groundwork, as well as quaint, history-haunted little towns and villages, and the Golden Fleece and Medea waiting at the other end of his voyage (after all, his middle name was Jason, and he called his car, an old Studebaker, Argo).

What made it so idyllic was the thought that Anne had told him on the phone that she loved him, and he began to envision a lifetime spent with her. *I'll propose marriage,* he thought, *not marriage now, of course, but somewhere down our lives' paths, something to look forward to, to plan for, to dream about.* After all, she was pinned to him. With such motivation, he could become anything—including a college English professor. Graduate school would be a trifle as long as he had a life with Anne to look forward to. He was teeming with thoughts, ideas, plans—a life of happiness and fulfillment. *What could possibly go wrong?* he confidently pondered.

Tobe's preoccupation on the trip was the future tense, full of hope and promise of a long life with Anne. He had told Anne that he would arrive either Friday or Saturday, so she may not have been expecting him this particular evening.

Tobe drove onto the campus of Meredith College just at dusk. He took in the old, dark redbrick, classic-looking buildings with a hint of Grecian influence. He knew that the campus, in summer and fall, was verdant and arbor laden, even though now the trees were stripped of their leaves. He viewed it as picturesque, hallowed, protective, and intellectually exploratory, the very embodiment of the achievement of Western learning and erudition and the university culture, which totally claimed him. Tobe was always moved by the, to him, sanctity of a college campus and its symbolic embodiment of his thirst for learning. He loved the place, and he and Anne had spent many an exciting and stimulating hour together under the ancient, wizened trees, reading poetry, discussing philosophy (especially Nietzsche, whom Anne favored most), and sharing personal thoughts. To him, ever the romantic, those memories embodied the sacredness of their relationship and their many adventures together. He was filled with anticipation and longed to see her once again.

Tobe pulled opened the large door of the dormitory where Anne lived and entered the looming lobby, which was dimly lighted. There were couches, love seats, lounge chairs, coffee tables, and furniture scattered around the expansive space. It was a Friday evening, and a common sight was several couples filling the spaces here and there, holding hands or even embracing. He adjusted his sight to the lack of lighting and then moved across the cavernous room to the receptionist's desk where a student worker sat reading Conrad's *The Heart of Darkness. Appropriate,* he thought.

"Hi," Tobe said. "I'm here to see Anne Sternbridge. Do you think you could page her?"

"She was just down here a while ago. I think she's still around here somewhere. She came down to study with a friend on one of the couches. You might go around and check to see if she's still here," the attendant suggested.

Tobe looked around but saw no one that looked like her.

"Why don't you circulate around. I think she's still here somewhere."

So Tobe started off to his right, examining various locations, and passed by a couch that was turned with its back to the rest of the room and that formed a little separate grouping in the corner with a coffee table and lounge chair. As he passed the couch, he noticed that there was a couple lying on the couch in a passionate embrace and engaged in some serious kissing. There was a boy in the topmost position and, as far as he could make out, a girl underneath, but Anne seemed to be nowhere in the room, so he returned to the receptionist's desk.

"Are you sure Anne is here?" Tobe asked the girl at the desk.

"Let me page her," the worker offered. She picked up the microphone and announced, "Anne Sternbridge, you are wanted at the front desk."

Tobe turned to look around the large lobby again, and to his astonishment, surreal as it seemed, the couple on the backward-facing couch stood up to reveal that it was Anne underneath the guy. Tobe's heart was doused in a wave of jealousy and anger. *Sonuvabitch,* Tobe thought, *she's got another boyfriend. This is unbelievable. I'm gonna kill somebody.* Tobe moved cautiously toward the couch.

"Anne? Is that you?" he said, with black thoughts on his mind.

"Tobe! I wasn't expecting you this evening!" Anne cringed.

"Apparently not. What the fuck is going on here?" Tobe said, purple with hurt, anger, and despair. He, being a peace-loving young man, was ready to attack, clenching and unclenching his fists and raising his arm instinctively as he approached the couple.

"Tobe. This is my friend Sarah," Anne said. Tobe stopped in silence and astonishment.

"Sa-sa-sa-rah?" he feebly repeated. Now he was even more dismayed, for Sarah was not a guy at all, and apparently Anne was unaware that Tobe had seen them. Sarah had a butch haircut, and there was no mistaking her gender preference.

"What are you guys doing?" Tobe asked.

"We're studying," Anne said.

Shall I tell her now what I saw, or shall I wait till later? Tobe debated, but all he could evince was "Studying what?" He was stunned, unable to find more words, and felt the coldest, brain-frozen numbness he had ever felt. He thought for a moment he might lose consciousness, swayed a little, and decided to sit down.

"The French Revolution," Anne stated simply.

French Revolution my ass, Tobe thought.

"Well," Anne said, "are you hungry?"

I couldn't eat if my life depended on it, Tobe thought. "I'm ravished," he lied. *What the hell do I do now? I'm totally lost.* Strangeness separated them.

"This is my friend Sarah," Anne said again.

"Nice to meet ya," Tobe mumbled, offering a limp hand.

"You too," Sarah said.

"Want to join us?" Anne asked Sarah.

"No, no. French Revolution exam Monday, you know. You guys have fun," Sarah said.

Tobe and Anne settled into a booth in an old, cheap Greek restaurant in downtown Raleigh. It was a dimly lit place with faded red plastic upholstery, checkered tablecloths, squeaky chairs, big band music out of the forties on the speaker system, and an extremely depressing ambiance (which, to Tobe, seemed appropriate), but the price was right and the food decent, in case anyone felt like eating.

"Anne? Do you like women more than men?" Tobe asked.

"What makes you ask that?"

"Can you answer my question?"

"Where is this coming from?"

"When I got to your dorm, I walked around in the lobby looking for you because I was told that you were there somewhere."

"Oh?"

"Yes."

And then there was silence.

Tobe could see Anne's mind crawling toward comprehension as her face began to redden, and then she said, "Oh."

"Right," Tobe said. "Oh."

And then another long silence followed.

"You saw?"

"Yes. I just assumed it was a couple—a boy and a girl—until the receptionist called you and you stood up. You want to know the funny part? I was livid because I thought you were with another guy. That tore my heart out. I was filled with jealously and rage and anger and—and. And then—well, imagine the turmoil in my heart then. I didn't know what to feel—except total and complete and utter despair and disorinetation and—"

He shrugged in stupefaction and inarticulateness.

"I'm sorry," she said.

"So. Do you like women more than men?" Tobe felt that it was a time for questions—and maybe even some honest answers.

More silence.

There are moments in one's life when one knows, even as it is happening, that it is a life-altering event, that it is a pivot, that it is directional, that things could change forever, never to be the same again, which he had experienced several times before in his young life. Tobe was not prepared to accept this new development as one of those moments as he held onto hope.

"Anne," Tobe said.

"Yes?"

"Will you marry me?"

"You're serious, aren't you?"

"Dead."

"How can you?" she said.

"We can beat this."

"You think?" she whispered, as though she had never thought of that.

"Love conquers all."

"Oh, Tobe. You are so precious."

"No, really, my love for you is so powerful it can cure anything."

"I—I—I'm totally lost," she said.

"I can't live without you. We can make this work. I want to spend the rest of my life with you. You're the only girl I have ever loved. I have women falling all over me all my life—beauty queens, high school superlatives, party girls, you name it, and I did not care a rat's ass about any of them because they were all so vacuous. You have substance. I'm so mesmerized by your intelligence, your knowledge, your depth, sensitivity—you're the only woman I want to be with."

"I care about you."

"Love, try the word love."

"I ..."

"You know, I think it would be better if you just told me that you hated me and be done with it. The way it is now, it just keeps me hoping." *Hopeless hope.* Tobe thought of Eugene O'Neill's philosophy of life.

"I ..."

"You said that already." Tobe was still trying to process the events of the evening and the present conversation. He felt as though he were dreaming for a moment or looking at the scene from a great distance. His first response was one of despair, but he shook it off, refortified himself, and drew upon his years of discipline in football, studying, and the struggles of being poor, beating all kinds of odds—as young as he was. He clung to his absolute love for her.

"Anne," he said, "you have some feelings for me. Right?"

"Of course."

"Okay. That's a start. I've already told you how I feel about you. It's not idle bullshit. It comes out of the very depths of my being. This is not the Tobe who plays the field here. That's all behind me. I'm on a new path to the future. This is Tobe the most sincere, earnest, honest, committed human being on this planet who is madly in love with you. Do you get that much?"

"Yes."

"I'm a man. You're a woman. Let's let nature take its course. Deep inside of you somewhere, you would prefer a man. It's only natural. You can overcome whatever it is you're dealing with. It's against nature. I'll be patient. I can wait. I'll be gentle with you, I'll take care of you, and I'll love you till the day I die."

Anne's face was deeply troubled, perplexed, and sweet.

"Will you marry me?" Tobe waited. "I don't mean right now but just make that commitment—for the future. We both have a long struggle ahead of us. School, career, searching, finding, exploring. But if down the road somewhere there was that prospect that we could spend the rest of our lives together, it would all be worth it."

The silence got louder, and Anne seemed to grow more pensive.

Finally, "Yes," she whispered. She looked up at him and beamed as though she had momentarily defeated some demon. She smiled, her face full of joy and tears.

"Why are you crying?" Tobe reached out to her.

"I don't know."

Tears of joy, Tobe hoped.

CHAPTER 5

Belhaven, North Carolina, Christmas Break, 1956

"Dad?" Tobe was in his bedroom where his dad had come in to visit with him about school and things in general. They had not had many father-son talks as of late, with Tobe away for most of the school year.

"Yeah?" His dad had found the dresser mirror in Tobe's bedroom and was preening, making sure everything was in place, especially his black, wavy hair, which now had specks of white in it.

"Can I ask you a question?" Tobe said.

"Sure." He could see his father's face in the large oval mirror. Tobe was lying in his bed when his father came in.

"I'm not quite sure how to put this—but—have you ever known a girl, er, woman, who seemed to like women more than she liked men?" Tobe wasn't sure he should be asking his father such a question.

"Why are you askin' me this?" His father turned away from the mirror and toward the bed.

"I'm just curious." Tobe propped himself up by putting his hands behind his head.

"Do you know somebody who does?" His father was now standing at the end of Tobe's bed.

"Does what?"

"Likes women more'n men."

"I'm not sure."

"If'n you do, stay away from her. I know from experience."

"You do?"

"Yes. Trust me. You'll never be able to change her mind. There are some women who prefer women more than men. I don't understand it, but it's a simple fact of life."

"Really?"

"There's a name for this kinda thing. It's called lai—something. Les—bian. That's it: lesbian," his dad said.

"Lesbian?"

"Yes. Don't go near her. You'll never have a chance. You ready to go out to dinner?"

"Sure. Let's go," he said as he swung his feet off the bed.

Anne had gone back for winter break to what was nominally and presently her hometown, White Mountain, North Carolina. They had agreed that Tobe would drive up to White Mountain, a short distance from Belhaven, while they were on break—as often as he could, which if Tobe had his way would be every day. The first such opportunity came the first weekend home for both of them. Tobe left Belhaven on a Saturday, midday, with admonishments from his parents about driving carefully, especially during the holidays, and arrived in White Mountain soon thereafter. Anne greeted him at the front door. Tobe became raptured again and gave Anne a loving hug as she pulled away.

"My parents are here in the living room," she said, holding his hand tenderly and leading him inside. Tobe had met her parents originally at the ESSO service station at the Crossroads in Belhaven when Tobe was giving Anne a ride back to school, the event that had germinated Tobe's attraction to Anne.

"I'm going to give Tobe a little guided tour of our teeming metropolis," Anne informed her parents as goodbyes were said, spattered with "drive carefully" and "dinner is at six" and "see you soon."

So Anne proceeded to give him a sightseeing excursion of their idyllic (if a person happened to be white) little town, once voted as an All-American City, whatever that meant, of which Anne was hypercritical.

"They're all a bunch of bigots," Anne said. "It's called White Mountain not because of the big rocky hill outside of town but because it's a white city. Let me show you how the other half lives."

Anne then proceeded to direct Tobe to what was referred to as Shanty Town "on the other side of the railroad tracks." Tobe was not unfamiliar with the conditions that southern coloreds had to live in and was always amazed by their incredible spirit and strength, even though he saw the conditions as worse than a third world country.

The streets were unpaved, composed mostly of North Carolina red clay with no sidewalks or drainage accommodations. The houses, if one wished to call them that, were shacks of various materials—tar paper, tin sidings, in some cases discarded billboard signs, and just about anything one could erect to create a shelter. Trash was scattered everywhere, an indication of course that there was no garbage collection and obviously no kind of sanitation system. Some houses had water wells with buckets hoisted above them, and some had outhouses, signs also that the "houses" had no plumbing. Colored kids, wearing rags for clothes, were playing in yards with sticks and rocks, with obviously no toys or trikes or bikes or wagons as would be seen in most neighborhoods. There were no parks or playgrounds with swings and slides or other amenities as would be found in white neighborhoods.

Of course Tobe, growing up in the old segregated South, had seen it all of his life and was rather immured to it, often delivering groceries into such neighborhoods, but this was the worst he had ever seen, and Anne was outraged. One of the things Tobe admired about Anne was that she had such a beautiful, caring, loving, altruistic, all-encompassing spirit that excited him. Her goodness was genuine, inclusive, and unifying: rich/poor, black/white, weak/strong, male/female, foreign/local, homo/hetero—it did not matter. Tobe knew that she cared for all human beings.

"We cannot let this continue," Anne said angrily. "Something has to be done. How can we let people live like this? What is wrong with us as a nation? How can we sleep at night?"

Tobe and Anne returned to Anne's parents' house. Tobe now had become comfortable enough to notice Anne's home. It was the parsonage (i.e., the preacher's house) of the First Baptist Church of White Mountain, located close to the church on the edge of the downtown area in an all-white neighborhood. Like the church, the mansion had tall white columns gracing the front of the house, a redbrick home with several stories.

Tobe did not bother to count the number of floors but sensed that it was a spacious place to live. The front door opened into a living area, which he had barely noticed upon his initial arrival, and spanned the whole length of the first floor, with deep-piled carpeting, gracious, overstuffed chairs and couches, rich, darkly colored wood breakfronts and secretaries, and heavy drapery. It epitomized elegance and gracious living, reflecting the essence of Mrs. Sternbridge. Elegance was the oxygen of her home, and Tobe wondered if Anne would be willing to exchange such luxury for his lack thereof. *Baptist preachers live well,* Tobe thought, and wondered fleetingly if he had made a mistake in rejecting the ministry.

And dinner was equally eloquent, after which Dr. and Mrs. Sternbridge retired to their bedroom, who knew how many floors up, and Anne and Tobe sat in the parlor off the living room. It was a cozy moment. Tobe was in Elysium Fields, as Emily Dickinson had suggested, and Anne seemed to try to be romantic with Tobe. She snuggled, she tried to be sexy, she worked at cuteness, and then she began to undress, first her sweater over her head, then her pants under her feet, and then everything else until she was nude, the second time in their history together.

"What about your parents!" Tobe said.

"They don't want to participate."

"Huh?"

"I invited them, but they insisted no."

So there they sat on the couch in the parlor, Tobe fully clothed and Anne with nothing on. It was not sexy. Tobe was embarrassed and did not know how to handle the situation. How could he tell her that this was not the way lovemaking proceeds?

"Don't you want me?" she said.

"Of course I do, but we have to sort of warm up to the moment. Don't you understand that?"

"Look. I'm spreading my legs. Isn't that what you want? Why don't you ravish me?"

"Oh geez."

"What?"

"Just let me hold you and kiss you and get excited first. I don't have a button I can push to make it happen," Tobe tried to explain.

"Do we have to?"

"Yes!"

"Okay. If we must."

Such an imposition, Tobe thought. *She has no idea. Is it her innocence or what?*

So Tobe tried to remind himself of how much he loved this person, which was an arousal argument, and tried to do a minimum of touchy-feely foreplay and then began to undress himself. *I do want her, God knows.*

He laid Anne gently down on the couch and placed himself between her spread-open legs and tried his best to make a beachhead but never succeeded. She seemed to resist with all her body, which seemed more like a wooden plank. This went on for a short while until Tobe stood up and declared, "It's no use."

"I'm not very good, am I?"

"I don't care. I love you like I have never loved another human being." Tobe looked around on the couch, grabbed his pants to cover his nakedness, and handed Anne her clothes.

"Let's get dressed," he said. *I am going to hate myself tomorrow.*

The next morning was Sunday, and off they walked to church, it being close by. Tobe and Anne accompanied Dr. Sternbridge to his Sunday school class, which he taught while Mrs. Sternbridge attended a senior women's group.

The minister greeted his class, welcomed the visitors, with special recognition of Tobe and Anne, and then asked Tobe to lead the class in a prayer. Tobe faked a sore throat, saying it was too painful to speak, and begged off. He had retired, in recognition of his life of the past, from leading public prayers. The preacher, after delivering a prayer, opened his Bible, announcing the passage as John 3:15–17, and began to read:

"'For God so loved the world that He gave his only begotten Son, that whosoever believeth in Him should not perish but have everlasting life. For God sent not his Son into the world to condemn the world; but that the world through Him might be saved,' the Gospel according to John," said Anne's father, Reverend Doctor Henry Hank Sternbridge. The Sunday school class was a senior men's Bible study class. He continued, "Later, Jesus says, 'In my Father's house are many mansions: if it were not so, I would have told you. I go to prepare a place for you. And if I go and prepare a place for you, I will come again and receive you unto myself that where I am, there ye may be also,' the fourteenth chapter of John, verses 2 and 3," and Anne's father concluded his scripture readings.

"What are we to make of this?" he said, looking around at the faces of the men in the class.

"It's poetry," a small female voice asserted from several rows back.

"Beg your pardon?"

"Jesus is just trying to put it into terms that the average person can understand. Everybody knows what a house is, so he compares heaven to a house, you know, a metaphor," the soft voice said.

"Huh, okay, that's one way of looking at it." Tobe could tell that the reverend was awkwardly trying to cover his daughter's refusal to be literal and move on.

"No it's not!" someone on the right side of the room said.

"I'm sorry?" the reverend said.

"The Bible is the Word of God, and every word in it is literally true—every period, every comma, every word is written by God, and we'll have none of this liberal, intellectual reading of God's sacred Word," said an old seemingly irascible, encrusted, Bible-thumping, hard-shell Baptist. Tobe was familiar with the type. "If God said it is a house, then it is literally a house. Period."

"Well, there are different ways of—"

"No! There's only one way—the Baptist way—and you better put a harness on your uppity daughter."

"All right, all right, everybody, let's all just take it easy." The minister tried to mollify the old man, to rein things in. Tobe looked at Anne in astonishment and admiration.

Anne stood up from her seat. "Okay, Mr. Jenkins, let me ask you one 0question." She turned to face him from across the room.

"Be my guest," he said.

"Jesus says that He has come so that, let's see"—she turned the pages of her Bible—"here it is: 'so that the world through Him might be saved.'"

"That's literally true," Jenkins said, assuring everyone.

"Okay. Good." She paused. "Does that include colored people?"

A gasp arose from the small gathering, and then there was silence while everyone turned to look at Harold Jenkins for his response.

"That's a different matter," Jenkins said.

"Are not Negroes a part of the world, literally speaking?" Anne said.

"They have their own church. I don't know what they teach over there."

"But we're talking about the Bible—God's Bible—and a literal interpretation of it."

"There is no room in this congregation for these liberal heresies about the Bible. I stand on the Bible foursquare, and I would think that the preacher's own family would do the same thing," Jenkins said as he stood to face her.

"What you should do is go over to Shanty Town. Have you seen it lately? Go over there and minister to those people who could use some help and some love," she said. Tobe knew there was a reason he loved her.

"I think it's time to move on," her father said, trying to harness the wild horse of a situation.

"I have another question for you, Mr. Jenkins," Anne said.

"It's a Bible study session. Go for it." Jenkins still defiantly stood.

"Jesus loves the whole world, right?"

"Right," he said as he played her game, unaware of the pitfall.

"Does that include homosexuals?"

"What!"

"Does Jesus love homosexuals? Homosexuals are a part of the world—'for God so loved the *world* that He gave His only begotten Son—'"

"They're all going straight to hell to suffer eternal damnation!"

"That's not what Jesus says."

"God is a just God, and He punishes people for their wickedness," Jenkins said.

"Jesus said, 'God is love,'" Anne said softly.

"And you're goin' to hell along with 'em!" Jenkins shouted.

"Let's try to be Christ-like at this moment," the reverend said calmly.

"Preach, you better set your own house in order before you try to lead your flock, and if you can't do that, then I think we may need another shepherd," Jenkins said as he banged himself down on his seat, looking satisfied with his performance. Tobe knew that he had indeed forcefully articulated a particular point of view—and that of many of those present. Tobe also understood why Anne had told him when they first met that she hated the South.

"Let's look at another passage." Her father's voice sounded weary and resigned.

In the past, Anne had told Tobe all about her relationship with her father and their numerous discussions, that she had questions, many questions, which she sometimes addressed with him. She said that he was a patient man but that she could tell her questions often disturbed him, saying that he knew the signposts of doubt when he encountered them, especially from someone who was his own flesh and blood. She told Tobe that her questions disturbed her as well, questions that she really did not want to be asking. They had a real bond on this subject because, Tobe confessed, he too had lots of unanswered questions and wondered aloud to her why he could not just accept the teachings of the Baptist Church and move on, but he could not. She said, like the poet she was, that she thirsted for the truth like a plow horse thirsts for water. Tobe was thinking about their past extended dialogues and contrasted it with Bettyjean's maniacal, blind religiosity.

Sunday brunch at the Sternbridge house, in spite of its elegance and style, was an extremely tense event, dominated mostly by silence. Anne's father apparently felt it wise not to discuss his Sunday school class at the table, mainly at the risk of upsetting his wife and ruining everyone's lunch. Tobe wondered if perhaps it would be best for him to point his compass toward Belhaven by midafternoon. But before lunch was over, Dr. Sternbridge proceeded to make an announcement.

"Before everyone leaves the table, I just want to tell you something: I think the time has come for me to start looking for another church—mainly outside the South." Tobe noted the various kinds of reactions around the table.

"Dad! Did I do something?" Anne said.

"No. I've been thinking about it for a while."

"But why, Hank?" his wife asked.

"I'm tired of being frustrated and angry."

"Jesus got angry too," Anne said.

"Yeah, I know. I stand up there and try to preach the love of Jesus, and all I get in return is hate talk. I just feel like I'm wasting my time."

"Where would we go?" Anne's mom asked.

"Don't know yet. I've been thinking I might even look for a faculty position at a seminary somewhere."

"I can relate to that," Tobe said.

"I'm proud of you, Dad," Anne said.

"There's a lot of trouble coming in the South. You can feel it. The colored folk are tired and getting impatient. All they want is fairness, their legal rights to be recognized as citizens. And they are right of course. All it's going to take is for a leader to come along to coalesce around, and I think one has already appeared on the horizon in Dr. Martin Luther King Jr. He's very young right now, but just wait. I can see it coming. We're in for some rough times. I think it's going to get pretty ugly before it gets better. End of sermon, so to speak." He rose from the table.

"Tobe," Anne said, "let's go for a ride."

Tobe was thinking about Anne's father's announcement and how it coincided with the one he had made regarding preaching versus teaching. He felt a kindred spirit with him.

"Tobe?" Anne put her hand on his arm.

"Sure. Let's go."

Tobe and Anne drove around for a long time, exchanging thoughts and grievances against injustice, and found themselves in total harmony, although Anne's thoughts on segregation and racial injustice were far more advanced and more militant than Tobe's, who had not given it all that much thought, although he clearly, judging by his demeanor, felt the wrongs.

"Tobe! See that dirt road that veers off to the right up ahead?" Anne asked.

"Yeah."

"Take it. Slow down. It's a little rough," she said.

They then drove up a hill on a rugged road flanked by a piney wood, came soon to the top of the ridge, then crested it and discovered on the other side an expansive valley with an enormous lake covering the expanse. It was the shortest day of the year, and the sun had passed its zenith and was midway down the sky, which was ablaze with glory. Tobe drove slowly on, headed toward the water's edge. Wintery day that it was, the place was deserted, seemingly primeval, and they relished their solitude. In a small clearing ahead, with a dock at the end of it extending over the water, Tobe eased into the patch of openness, secured the car, murdered the engine, and turned to Anne.

"Edenic," Tobe said.

"You like my place?" Anne asked as she began shedding first her sweater and then her blouse.

"What are you doing?"

"Isn't this what you want?" She continued with her pants.

"Why do I always get the feeling that you're just trying to be a good sport?"

"Well, we're boyfriend and girlfriend, aren't we? I just want to please you."

"I would be happy to just hold you and kiss you and take things easy and naturally. I always feel like you're forcing things," he said.

"Why does there have to be all this hugging and kissing?"

"Because that's the way it's done between a man and a woman. That's part of the—uh—pleasure." Tobe still found himself trying to explain sex to her.

"Come on, Tobe. Take your clothes off."

Tobe slipped his sweater over his head, unbuttoned his shirt, and removed it. Anne watched. After he got his trousers off, what followed was another charade of impenetrableness; Tobe was torn between forcing the issue or being gentle. He chose gentleness, so they put their clothes back on and sat in silence until finally Tobe spoke.

"You know that metaphor you used about dancing on horses as a way of describing race relations in the South?"

"Yes."

"Our attempts at lovemaking are like that."

"How so?"

"It's like we're standing on two different horses, and we're trying to dance with each other, but the horses are bouncing us up and down, and we can barely hang on, and the horses are moving at different speeds and trying to pull away from each other, and we just can't get synchronized. We can't even get close to each other. It's impossible to dance with each other as long as we're on two different horses, but it would be a lot easier if at least we were on the same horse, or if we weren't on horses at all." Tobe felt relieved.

"Dancing on horses might describe the whole relationship," Anne said.

"Maybe so. I think I should return to Belhaven now," Tobe said.

Damnation! Tobe's language, since giving up on being a preacher, had become more expressive of his feelings. *Or damned. That's more like it. I feel damned—or—cursed—or tortured! I've never loved anyone the way I love this woman. And yet it's like we're on two different planets—or horses.*

"What are the names of the horses?" Anne asked.

"You tell me," Tobe said.

The Epiphany: The Names of the Horses

If the drive from Belhaven to White Mountain the day before on Saturday had been one in sunlight accompanied by great joy and eagerness for Tobe, the drive back from White Mountain to Belhaven on Sunday late afternoon was one in the dimness of last light, depression, and pensiveness.

Something just isn't right, Tobe thought as he drove toward Belhaven, *and I just can't figure it out. Is it me? I certainly had no problems with Gail—or last summer when I was a lifeguard—with Charlene or Norma or all the others. If it's not me, then it must be Anne. What is it about her?*

And then a flashback cracked his brain open, a picture of Anne and her girlfriend making mad, passionate love on the couch in the dorm lobby. It was a painful but clear image. *She certainly had no trouble kissing her friend. Oh shit,* Tobe thought. As he drove along, he topped a hill and saw in the eventide light a beautiful horizon in the distance and thought of O'Neill's play *Beyond the Horizon.* He thought, *Yes, I am going to move on beyond the horizon where another world awaits me, unknown, mysterious but full of possibilities—and the past and all its pain will disappear after I cross the horizon.*

Tobe arrived home in a state of despair, confusion, and doubt. But of one thing he was sure. *The names of the horses are Hetero and Homo, and the two will never be able to dance. I have fallen madly in love with a lesbian. My life is ruined.* And so it came to pass.

EPILOGUE

After Tobe graduated from college, Anne had one more year left and graduated the following year. Both Tobe, with his philosophy major, and Anne, with her literature major, had lost their life compasses and were without direction. Without any clear goal in mind and for no particular reason, Anne applied to Union Theological Seminary, the home of God, in New York City. Tobe's young philosophy professor had graduated from Union, had studied under the famous theologian Paul Tillich and other notable theologians at Union, and found direction and purpose in his life thereat, and Tobe had shared with Anne many encomia and narratives about his fabulous philosophy professor. *Ergo*, concluded Anne, *perhaps that is a place where I can find myself and (or) God*. Such a decision did not displease her minister father either. She was accepted into Union for the academic year 1959/60 and commenced her studies there in the fall. She had always been a brilliant student and had no trouble mastering the intricacies of theological thought and passing exams and papers but found no secret keys to unlocking her own life and began to despair of ever doing so.

In March 1960, a young African American minister from Alabama came to address the student body at Union, among whom sat Anne Sternbridge—in the front row. His name was Martin Luther King Jr., and the Montgomery, Alabama, bus boycott had elevated his name onto front-page headlines across the land. Everyone, as history soon established, was familiar with the sparkling oratorical skills of Dr. King, and he cast a hypnotic spell over the entire student body, including a young female theological student eagerly taking notes.

Dr. King described at great length the blight on African Americans in the South, the injustices, the abuses, the wrongs, the violence, the living nightmare that was their lives. His descriptions were deeply moving and powerful. But Dr. King did more than that—he offered a solution.

Yes, there would be protests and demonstrations and battles and hard times fighting for the right to vote, to participate in the American dream as equals, to pass legislation and make laws, to gain access to equal education, to fully implement democracy for all people.

And then he unfolded his special philosophy and told the story of how Mahatma Gandhi broke the back of the mighty English empire with his philosophy of nonviolence and used Gandhi as his model for the civil rights movement. King intended to put the principles of Jesus into action, the principles of love and peace. Anne, by the appearance on her face, seemed to have an epiphany, and after his presentation, she rushed over to where Dr. King was surrounded by a small crowd.

"Dr. King," Anne said to the young minister after waiting interminably for others to have their chance to speak to him and bless him. King then turned to her and said, "Hello."

"My name is Anne Sternbridge, and my father is a Baptist minister in the South who has been fighting against hatred and prejudice all his life, and I know now that I must dedicate myself to the same cause."

"That's very nice of you," the patient, young King said.

"I mean it with all my heart."

"Well, when you finish your theological studies—"

"No!" she said.

"Excuse me?"

"I am not waiting. I mean right now. This minute. What can I do? How can I help?"

"Well, er—aren't you in school right now?"

"I am quitting school as of this moment, and I am going back to the South to start working for the cause. Where do I start?" She was as ever, as Tobe knew all too well, impetuous.

"You're serious, aren't you?"

"As serious as I have ever been in my life about anything."

Dr. King took a business card and his pen out of his pocket and wrote on it.

"Here," he said, "this is the name of a lady in Georgia who is organizing students to help start the movement. Give her a call. Tell her that I gave you her number, and she'll tell you what you can do."

Anne looked at the card and, just to be sure, read the name out loud. "Ella Baker."

"Yes, the most loving, caring woman you'll ever meet and a real organizer. She has plans, and she's making things happen," Dr. King explained.

Astonishingly and swiftly, Anne went to the registrar's office the next day to announce her withdrawal from school, packed her belongings in her '58 Chevy, took her car out of the garage located next to Columbia University, which was located next to Union Theological Seminary just below Harlem, and headed south on Fifth Avenue.

She would keep going south until she reached the South, Atlanta specifically, in April 1960, just when the civil rights movement was a little more than embryonic. It had begun as a sit-in by four black students in Greensboro, North Carolina, in a Woolworth's five-and-dime at the lunch counter. They, of course, were refused service, and so they were determined to sit on those stools at that counter until they were served.

Anne had arrived in the South just in time to make her contribution in any way she could. She presented herself at the address she had been given, and there she met Ella Baker, who as a friend of Dr. King's was a leader in the Southern Christian Leadership Conference and was making other organizational plans, one of which was to begin to organize students, those who were the promise of the future.

"I hope you know what you're getting yourself into," Miss Baker warned Anne.

"Oh, yes, ma'am, I think I do," Anne said.

"There's goin' to be some ugliness up ahead."

"That's all right too, Miss Baker." Anne stood unflinchingly.

"'Specially for a white girl."

"I understand."

"I's organizin' a new group 'specially for students. Would you be interested?" Miss Baker asked.

"Anywhere you can use me."

"We only have a couple of students right now. If you join us, you can be the secretary. Everybody is an officer."

"I'm in," Anne said.

And her destiny was set. Anne's journey toward meaning in her life and in her search for God was found in the beleaguered, abused African American faces of the South. "Inasmuch as ye have done it until the least of these, My brethren, ye have done it unto Me." Would she finally be able to dance on horses?

Belhaven, North Carolina, Summer, 1957

"Dad." Tobe, standing in the little hall outside of their bathroom, addressed his father, who was peering into the bathroom mirror while shaving, white foam covering the lower half of his face. Tobe was standing in the same place he had stood ten years before when he had tried to ask what "they" meant by "being saved."

"Yep?"

"Can I ask you a question?" Tobe said.

"Shoot."

"Did you—have you—ever reached a point in your life when you didn't know where you were going next?" Tobe did not really know why he was asking his father such a vague question and did not really understand what kind of answer he wanted. He just felt he needed help, strengthening, direction, something at a bleak moment in his life.

Tobe had graduated from the university in the spring of 1957 with his beloved philosophy major, without a path as to how to get to his predetermined destiny to be a college English professor. In desperation, he had investigated the possibility of graduate work in philosophy, unable to think of another viable option, by visiting Emory University in Atlanta. He was in fact accepted into their program but without a scholarship, a grant, a teaching assistantship, or any means of financial support in graduate school. After graduation, he had gone with some buddies to sell Bibles in New Jersey but soon called his parents, asking his parents for bus fare to come home, which was the situation he was in on this Sunday morning as he watched his father shaving. He had retrieved his old job as lifeguard, now a hollow commitment, but he knew that it was only a temporary thing and that decisions had to be made soon.

"Do you remember when I was working in the hosiery mill?" his father asked.

"Of course," Tobe replied.

"And remember when I said that I could not go on with that job—that I was getting too old for it and I needed to find something else?"

"Sure do."

"I mean, I was making good money as far as millwork was concerned, but the job was killing me, and I just could not go on."

"I remember."

"And so I quit, without a clue as to what I was going to do next and a family to support. It was a tough time in my life," his dad confessed.

"So how did you handle it?"

"I got down on my knees, and I asked God to help me—and he did."

"I'm kind of in that situation now."

"Start praying—that's all I can tell you," he said.

Tobe was aware that he was at a crucial juncture in his life, which at first felt like he was carrying a two-ton weight in the dark, an awesome responsibility that depressed and nagged at him. He wandered away from his dad and into his bedroom and shut the door. He started meditating about his situation, and then suddenly he thought about what he had learned in his study of existentialism, which was that the meaning of life is in the living of it, and meaning is found in the decisions we make, that every choice we make creates the pattern of our existence, and that pattern is the meaning of our lives. He suddenly felt excited, even exhilarated because he now understood that his life was in his hands and his alone, that he depended on no one to make his life complete, that being alone, on his own, and being his unique self was all that was required. He felt empowered, and he understood that what lay before him was an unlimited future that he was in charge of and that his chief duty was to actualize his true potential as a human being. The God within him had spoken and would be his guide from this point forward. He also decided to give up trying to dance on horses and to dance on solid ground instead.